T0163211

THE IMAGE

A NOVEL IN PIECES

Steven Faulkner

BEAUFORT
BOOKS

THE IMAGE

Hardcover ISBN: 9780825309762
Ebook ISBN: 9780825308543

For inquiries about volume orders, please contact:
Beaufort Books
27 West 20th Street, Suite 1102
New York, NY 10011
sales@beaufortbooks.com

Published in the United States by Beaufort Books www.beaufortbooks.com
Distributed by Midpoint Trade Books, a division of Independent Book Publishers
www.midpointtrade.com
www.ipgbook.com

Book design by Mark Karis

Printed in The United States

For artists Andrea and Jake

CONTENTS

The Word unheard,
The Word without a word, the Word within
The world and for the world;
And the light shone in darkness and
Against the Word the unstilled world still whirled
About the centre of the silent Word.

—FROM "ASH WEDNESDAY"

T. S. ELIOT

IKON

The year: AD 755, more than 100 years after the Battle of Yarmouk drove the Byzantine armies back upon their capital of Constantinople and allowed Muslims to control Damascus, Aleppo, and areas south and west.

+ + +

A bearded monk reclines on one elbow in the shadows of tall pine trees near the gate of an old stone Maronite monastery built on a remote ridge of the southern Lebanese mountains. The monk has been watching a cricket make its complicated journey across the thatch of dry pine needles beneath the ancient pines; slowly, methodically, it steps over the long dry needles, ducking beneath clumps, climbing over an occasional twig or broken limb, pausing, lifting and swinging its antennae this way and that. The old monk picks up a stick and pokes at the cricket. It jumps onto a flagstone, part of a walkway that passes under an arched stone gateway and climbs a gentle rise to a low-roofed building constructed of rough field stones and roofed with timbers and red clay tiles.

Few travelers climb the trail to this poor mountain monastery, so the old monk is surprised by movement on the dirt trail below. A figure is walking up through scattered pines and oaks. The day is hot, the sun high. The monk slowly pulls his thick fingers through his long, greying beard, watching what appears to be a young man or a boy plodding up the dirt trail, a sack over his shoulder. The monk's hand slides beneath his considerable paunch, lifts it from the pine needles and absently lets it fall back. His old eyes aren't as clear as they used to be, but he soon sees that the climber, except for the sack over his shoulder, is naked. The monk runs a hand over his balding head, then reaches for the limb above him and hoists himself to his feet, still watching the thin body passing in and out of tree shadows, hobbling up the dirt path, lugging that heavy sack.

The old monk steps to the flagstones to block the arched gateway. He clasps his big hands firmly across his stomach and calls out, "Why do you shame us by coming naked to the house of God?"

The boy stops and takes a long look at the grey-bearded monk in his dark robe.

The monk can see the boy's laddered ribs and concave stomach in the sunlight, moving in and out, panting from the effort of climbing.

The boy lets the sack slide from his shoulder and drop with a clatter to the path. He rubs his shoulder and calls out, "Robbed . . . I was robbed."

"But not of your bag?"

"I carry rocks."

"Rocks?"

"Small rocks."

"Our house is made of rocks. Why do you bring us more?"

"Beautiful rocks."

The monk takes his hand and with one thick finger strokes the sweat from his eyebrows. "Beautiful?"

The boy nods.

"What are we to do with beautiful rocks?"

The boy says nothing, squinting up at the old monk.

"You are hungry, boy?"

"Yes."

"How long since you have eaten?"

"Three days."

"No food for three days?" The monk clasps his hands beneath his paunch.

"I found some fig trees in the mountains," the boy says. "Along the stream. I ate dried figs."

"And still you lug the rocks?"

"Yes."

"Your nose is smashed and swollen; you carry a wound on your forehead."

The boy's fingers touch the thick scab on his forehead. "The thief," he says. "But he let me live so he could ask me about the rocks."

"The rocks."

The boy nods. "Twice. He hit me twice and could have killed me, but he also was curious about the rocks."

"Ah! Then let me see these precious rocks."

+ + +

The sun moves through the needled pines toward the western mountains as the boy sorts the polished pebbles by color on the flagstones.

Flat, roughly polished pebbles the size of ordinary Roman coins or Greek drachmas, some much smaller. He collects them by color. The boy has words for the colors: "red cow, sparrow speckle, Antioch wine, Athenian white, baked bread, burnt bread, old cream, fresh cream, rain-cloud dark, rain-cloud light, August grass, morning sky, pale horizon, starry evening, starry night . . ."

The fat monk has forgotten the boy is naked. Squatting beside the trail, he keeps plucking flat pebbles the boy has sorted, holding them to the sun, raising an eyebrow, waiting for the boy to call out its name: "lizard green . . . lizard-tail blue." A few are quartz crystals or shiny obsidian, some are sea-green amethysts, but most are various shades of white, brown or grey, pale ocher, or limestone yellow, not remarkable.

"What is this? A soft rock?" The monk holds it up.

"A dried fig."

"My name is Brother Barnabos," the monk says as he pops it into his mouth, feels it with his tongue, then chews. "Not much taste." He points to three heavier rocks stacked together on the dirt path.

"Grinding stones: rough, medium, smooth."

Brother Barnabos picks up a leather sack with pebbles glued to its surface.

"Smalti," says the boy. He pauses. "And my mother's necklace."

"Smalti?"

"Squares of gold foil sealed in thin squares of glass and other squares of colored glass."

"The thief missed this sack?"

"It was sundown and the rocks glued to the leather disguised it."

"Clever boy," says the monk. "But why do you lug rocks up mountain trails?"

The boy is on his knees sorting the last of the pebbles. He pauses. "We are in Muslim lands here?"

"The Caliphate appoints our civil rulers, but most of the people in these mountains are Christians. The officials leave us to practice our faith, cut timber, make wine, prune our olive trees, say our prayers, but we pay them for the privilege."

"The emperor has no authority here?"

"Byzantium has had no authority here for a hundred years."

The boy nods.

"Why do you ask?"

"What does your abbot think of ikons?"

Barnabos glances quickly through the gate, then back at the naked boy.

+ + +

Dressed in ragtag clothes from the monastery's supply for beggars, the boy sits at table with thirty monks eating flatbread with lentil and leek soup and pieces of strong goat cheese. He has twice drained the tall ceramic cup of its water. A young monk moves along the tables with a large pitcher of water. There is a heavy murmur of conversation beneath the long, low-beamed ceiling, the smell of the soup and of unwashed bodies, the occasional laugh. Ten monks at his table glance at him from time to time, but before the boy finishes devouring the meal, the monks stand for evening prayers and chant a lengthy hymn in a lonely minor key.

The boy waits. Tears come to his eyes, for the haunting melody and the words of the Psalm remind him of a day when his father walked with him and his older brother to a monastery east of the coastal Byzantine city of Ephesus, where they had listened to the monks sing.

When the hymn ends, he returns to the flatbread and cheese, wiping the last of his bread around the bottom of the empty soup bowl, then he rises to stand with the monks as the abbot leads them in evening prayers.

+ + +

They sit in the morning sun on boulders to one side of the main building: the fat monk Barnabos, the boy, the middle-aged abbot. A shallow meadow below them cups a pond. Below the pond, willows and pines flank a small rippling stream that wanders down the meadow and away into the forest.

The abbot asks the boy about his origins, why he, a Greek speaker, is traveling alone through these mountains controlled by the Muslim Caliphate, what his intentions are. The boy tells him of a visit to these mountains when he was young.

The abbot's face is thin, deep lines mark the corners of his mouth, dark eyebrows crowd his eyes, his greying hair hangs loosely about his shoulders. The abbot gazes out across the meadow at fenced vegetable gardens that follow the stream. "Your father was wealthy? Taking time to visit the mountains?"

"He was collecting materials for work."

"And what materials did he find in these mountains?"

"Rocks."

The abbot pulls at his moustache. "He was a builder?"

"He was a maker of ikons."

The abbot glances sharply at the boy. "But years ago, your Christian emperor Leo banished the making of ikons."

"My father worked for the bishop of Ephesus."

The abbot takes a deep breath and nods. "Of course, that bishop allows the old idolatries to continue." He glances again at the boy. "You must know that the emperor's son, Constantine the Fifth, is now enforcing the laws against such pagan worship of images."

"We do not worship the ikons," the boy says.

"Divinity," continues the abbot, "cannot be pictured. God is invisible spirit."

"The Christ was visible," says the boy.

A file of monks carrying hoes and spades walks past the three, following a path down to the fenced vegetable gardens.

"My father," says the boy, "told me that since the appearing of the Son of God, we may use material things to image the body of the Christ and of the saints and the martyrs. That Christian artists have been making images since the persecutions of Nero in the first century, maybe before. There are painted Christian frescoes from long ago in the caves beneath Ephesus of St. Paul, of Thecla, and of the Holy Virgin."

"An early corruption of our holy faith. Your father could read?" The morning sun is bright, and the abbot puts up a hand to shield his eyes so he can look at the boy.

The boy says, "My father read John of Damascus."

"Of course," says the abbot. "That man was able to promote his heresy because, like us, he lived among the Muslims and the emperor could not touch him. You also can read?"

"My father taught me."

"You have read the Scriptures? No graven images!" The abbot's voice is controlled but emphatic. "A lifeless image records only a physical shape of the Christ, not the divine. We

7

do not follow the heretic Nestorians who say that the Son of God was composed of two separate persons, one divine and the other human. He is one person."

"With two natures," says the boy.

"Yes. With two natures: true man and true God, but one person. You cannot portray the divine with rocks or paint, only the human, thus you separate the indivisible God into two."

"Two natures in one person," says the boy, "we form the person."

"You cannot portray the living God with lifeless rocks!"

"My father's images are not lifeless." The boy's eyes are suddenly fierce.

The abbot takes another deep breath and forces a smile. "The dead rocks come alive, I suppose."

The boy looks away across the meadow and beyond the pond to where several donkeys graze, and beyond them a herd of goats wanders the meadow, switching their short tails, and beyond them the forests and the peaks of blue mountains. There comes a faint tinkling of bronze bells. Two of the younger monks walk up the path toward them carrying wooden buckets of water from the stream.

"God can make even the rocks speak," says the boy.

"You have had conversations with these rocks?" The abbot smiles.

"Did not our Lord himself say that if the people would not praise God, the very stones would cry out?"

The old monk Barnabos has been sitting in silence. He glances sideways at the boy.

The abbot sighs and looks away. "But here," says the abbot, "we men *do* praise the Divine One, morning, noon, and evening.

Thus we encourage the rocks to keep their mouths shut."

"And even the hills and mountains will shout for joy," says the boy, his voice rising, "the forests sing and the seas roar."

"You are a little theologian?" The abbot smiles again. He pulls a nearby stem of seeded grass and begins chewing the stem. "Images are idols. They are forbidden. At best, they are mere symbols."

"As are words," says the boy.

"What is your name, boy?"

"Kostas."

"Kostas, we will not have ikons here. The emperor himself sends an annual contribution of gold to this monastery because he knows that I keep to the ancient and true faith and will not permit statues or images of any kind."

The boy is about to object to this, but Barnabos interrupts. "The boy is young, Tomas. He needs time to absorb new teachings. It is natural for him to believe his own father."

The abbot takes the grass stem from his mouth. "Well said, Brother Barnabos. We will give the boy time. And where is your father?"

"My father joined monks who were protesting the new laws against ikons. They arrested him with several monks. When the officers found out he was the bishop's ikonographer, they executed him."

The abbot frowns and looks down. "I am sorry, young Kostas, for you and your family. I do not judge your father for walking according to his conscience. But we are men of peace. You need not fear us." The abbot looked away across the meadow and pond. "Nevertheless, I will not allow ikons in this place."

+ + +

The rush and fall of a mountain stream swirls and plunges down a ravine at the foot of a steep-shouldered mountain cluttered with boulders and brush on one side while a mountain forest climbs the opposite slope, fringing the skyline with ancient cedar groves, occasional pines, and brushy, rocky ridges. The sunlight is intense. The morning air, chill.

A thin ten-year-old boy lies stomach down on a large, smooth boulder that breaks the current and leaves a quiet swirl of clear water behind. The boulder beneath his stomach is cool, but sunlight lies warm on his back.

He reaches a hand into the cold water of the shallow eddy and lifts a pebble between thumb and forefinger. He looks at the smooth grey stone and holds it up for his father to see.

His father is dressed as usual in the simple linen of a common worker; his more elegant, deep-blue cloak that marks his official position is folded into the crook of a nearby oak. His greying hair is pulled back from a deeply tanned forehead and tied at the back of his neck; his beard is shaved off in the old Roman fashion. He squats ankle-deep in the clear circling eddy, quickly sorting small stones, even tiny ones, and flipping the chosen ones onto a long strip of faded rag lying along the gravel shore.

The boy shouts over the hoarse rush of whitewater, "This one?"

His father glances up at the sound of his son's voice and looks at the pebble in the boy's fingers. "Too fat. Flat. Flatter. If it is too round, we must grind it down. Too much work for your older brother." His father smiles, and his long fingers dart back into the water, finding by feel the right ones, lifting each to inspect the color, discarding many, flicking the chosen ones into separate piles on the length of rag according to color: ochre, red-brown, black, cream, and many shades of grey. "We need more blackbirds, and anything snow, even dirty snows, but grey birds like that are fine too. Any color is a gift, but let them be thinner, more ground down by trouble."

"By trouble?" The boy sits up.

His father smiles.

A cool breeze is slipping over the forested ridge and rustling down through the shoreside bushes. The boy catches the scent of mountain pines. He listens to the whispering leaves and the raucous stream and the sudden chitter of a swooping kingfisher. He loves these mountain excursions away from the busy clatter of passing carts, the braying of donkeys, shouts of children and men, the rush and stink of city life. He slides off the boulder and steps through icy water to shore, where he looks for flatter pebbles in the dry gravel. Finding one, he holds it up. His father sees him, nods, and calls, "Dip it in the water first and look at the colors, then find the right pile on the rag."

The boy wets it and looks at the darkened grey stone flecked with white and yellow.

His father says, "You see? The stones come alive."

+ + +

The smell of carefully mixed, fine-sand mortar. The boy is fifteen now, and he sits beside his older brother on the stone floor ten meters below his father on the scaffold above. The mid-morning sun slants from a high circular window in the elaborate Basilica of Saint John, a two-hundred-year-old church resting on a hill above the old city of Ephesus. The sunlight illumines a wide circle of the interior wall where his father works. Quick fingers sort through piles of flat, polished stones laid out on the board at his feet by color. One hand holds a stone to the sunlight, then drops it back into a pile. Finding a piece, he presses it into fresh mortar to continue the shading of what looks to be a fold of white linen. "Grind this corner." He drops a stone to his older son seated below, who catches it and begins grinding the edge against a piece of granite between his knees. His father keeps sorting pieces. "More milks, Kostas," he says to the fifteen-year-old. Kostas reaches out to the pile of whites and picks up two, tossing them up to his father. His father swipes them out of the air, then lays them on the wood plank. "Those will work later, but I need five of the Athens marble, the white sparkle."

Outside, a dog barks.

They stop and listen. Just a single yip, so they continue their work.

"The emperor," says their father, "is sending soldiers to destroy ikons in the cities. I heard this news from three men coming down from Constantinople early this morning. After we finish our work here, we will move far east and south into the mountains near the Melkites or Maronites where we sometimes gather stones. Maybe near one of the monasteries."

"Leave home?" asks young Kostas.

"Move into the lands of the Muslim Caliphate?" The older boy looks alarmed.

"There will be no work for us here. And to anger the emperor of the Byzantine Empire . . ."

The dog outside barks, several sharp barks.

The older boy stands up and looks toward the doorway. "Why are we still working if this is the law? They will punish us. There is a rumor that the emperor himself rubs oil into the beards of ikon-loving monks and sets their faces on fire!"

"I have heard the rumors."

"They may be true."

"They may be true," says their father.

The older boy sits back down. "He made the patriarch of Constantinople ride backwards and naked on a black donkey through the city streets because he refused the edicts against ikons. You know this is true, Father."

"We have been paid. Justice requires us to complete this work. We build here three ikons of the great saint John Chrysostom."

"Why is the first image naked, standing with his back to us?" Kostas asks.

"Because Chrysostom once said, 'Do you wish to honor the body of Christ? Do not ignore him when he is naked.' He said this in defense of the poor. So, I have formed him naked. The second image, as you see, has him robed as a priest, as he was when he lived in Antioch. The third that we now create has him robed as patriarch of Constantinople. He was a brave man, boys, speaking against the luxuries of the rich and making an enemy of the emperor's wife. We honor his courage with these stones."

The older boy tosses the ground piece to his father, who presses it precisely between two pale grey pieces. He glances at Kostas, then catches, one at a time, the five pieces of white marble as the boy tosses them up.

The older boy looks again to the doorway, his curly blond hair now catching a ray of the rising sun. "The military commander Michael Lachanodrakon attacks monasteries that hold ikons, Father. You know this is true."

Their father keeps working.

Young Kostas tosses up another white stone. "You make him

naked to honor the patriarch who rode the donkey, don't you? The figure stands with his back to us, looking over his shoulder."

The father glances quickly down at his fifteen-year-old son.

The steady rising of the sun moves the warm patch of light down the wall as the father works so that he squats down to hold each piece in the sunlight before applying it to the mosaic. The older boy occasionally stands up and walks to a pot of mortar which he stirs with a stick, sometimes adding a little water. He looks up at his father and says, "I think we should obey the emperor."

"Are you afraid, Loukas?" their father asks.

"Of course. It is wise to fear the emperor."

"Yes." But his father keeps sorting and placing each sparkling piece of white marble along the ridge of the sleeve to catch the light.

✦ ✦ ✦

She sits on a cushion, her back against the wall of their sleeping room. Her face is drawn and anxious. She sips a cup of wine and motions for Kostas to sit.

He finds a cushion, sits, and asks his mother, "So you will marry this old man Demetrius?"

"Yes! Of course I will marry good Demetrius. You cannot support me. No one pays ikonographers anymore. Your father was most fortunate to keep working this long. Now that your father is gone, perhaps Demetrius can find you work in the city administration. His cousin is a decurion."

"I must do my own work."

"I knew you would say that." She looks into the small, shaded courtyard of their home. She sets the cup of wine on the tile floor, reaches behind her neck, opens the clasp of her necklace, and hands it to her son.

He takes the ruby pendant in his hand.

"This your father gave me on our wedding day. He told me it was his heart written in stone. You know how he loved the colored stones. This was the richest gift he could find for me."

Kostas looks at the dark ruby and lifts it toward the light, a rich, translucent red clasped in a thin gold ring. He examines the delicate braid of gold links. "But it's yours, my mother."

"After they murdered your father, we are all seen as enemies. You know this. It is a miracle that old Demetrius will take me as his wife. You are now a young man, the son of a well-known ikonographer, and they will hunt you here in Ephesus. Demetrius is sympathetic to you and to your work, but after Bishop Cosmos was sent into exile, we have no one to protect us, and the emperor's officers will make you take the oath against the making of ikons. I know you. You will not so betray your father and our faith. We have no word from your brother Loukas since he joined the army and went north to fight the Slavs. Since the army supports Constantine the Fifth, Loukas may be shielded from danger. But you must flee. You must flee south into Muslim lands as your father planned for us and find a monastery or church that will make use of your great skill, Kostas."

She stops her rapid instructions and leans back against the wall, picking up the wine cup and putting it to her lips. "Do you remember when the bishop gave us money to travel to Athens to find stones for the cathedral ikons, Kostas?" She smiles and closes her eyes.

"Yes."

"Those were days of gold. You were such a little boy that year, bouncing about like a goat, looking for rocks, so excited when you found one to please your father."

She opens her eyes. "This ruby is your father's heart and your mother's heart, Kostas. I want you to take it with you. But if you must sell it for food, sell it. I have no money to give you. They took everything but your father's old, worn-out rags. They would not touch the smalti. Perhaps they think the very materials of ikons are evil. You must take those with you."

"I will never sell this necklace."

"Don't say that, Kostas. Live! You must live! Send word to me from the mountains so that I also may live. And Kostas, you are a fine ikonographer. You have the passion your father had as a young man, but you have more talent. I could not tell you this while your father lived. You must continue this work. Perhaps south in Muslim lands you will find a monastery that will allow you to complete your vocation. The old monks are faithful and true Christians. They still make the holy ikons."

The boy fingers the ruby and watches his mother's face.

+ + +

He walks alone along a trail that skirts a mountain stream, climbing south into the mountains, his eyes always returning to the shallow-water stones, noting the colors, scanning the landscape so he can place the location of each change in rock layers, the shades of yellow-white on the outcroppings above, a thin edge of hard black, even blue-green shale scattered down a slope.

Across the stream he notices an outcropping of raw, yellow-white marble. He carries an old sack of faded blue made of one of his father's worn-out robes. It is filled with flat pebbles. Wading into knee-deep water, he leans over to pick up small pebbles of marble. "Caliphate yellow," he says.

+ + +

The sun has already passed beyond the mountain ridge when a man in a hooded robe steps from a crevice in the walls of the shadowed cliff. Kostas turns toward the sound of sandals on gravel as the man swings a thick walking stick that bounces off Kostas' head.

+ + +

His eyes open to darkness. There is a stench. Some dead animal. His fingers move slowly to his forehead, the caked blood and swelling above his left eyebrow. He finds that he is naked. Even his sandals are gone. The night sky is broken only by scattered stars above the opposite mountain slope. His eyes move to the nearby cliff for signs of movement. A cool wind is blowing down the mountain, and he is cold.

His hand reaches out to find the bag he was carrying and touches a small flat stone. Then another, and another. He rolls onto his stomach and draws his knees under him. His head is throbbing. He starts crawling down the trail, gathering the stones in the dark, but there are too many and his head is a blinding pain. He turns his head and vomits.

+ + +

His eyes open. He sits up shivering and groans, cups the swelling on his forehead, touches the clotted blood with his fingers, and listens to the mountain stream. He presses his strong fingers into the muscles above his ears and at the base of his neck, trying to rub away the pain. The mountain to the east is a black silhouette against a slowly dawning sky. The stars have faded.

He notices with a start a small man wrapped in a robe sitting with his back to the layered limestone wall of rock that rises abruptly from the trail. The man's face is hidden beneath the hood of his robe, but his thick beard catches the faint light.

The beard moves: "Why do you carry rocks?"

Kostas takes a breath and glances up the trail and turns to look down the trail. No one in sight. "I like rocks."

"No one carries useless rocks through the mountains," says the little man.

A small breeze stirs the nearby grasses and the stench returns.

"I like rocks. My father taught me."

"Taught you to like useless stones."

"Why did you hit me?"

"You carried a heavy bag. I expected more than common rocks."

"There was bread and cheese too."

"I ate it. And a small skin of wine. Very good. I have slept here, waiting for you to recover from your little nap so we could have a pleasant conversation. It seems you ate rotted goat meat; I saw you vomit."

Kostas stares at the little man. "I am sick. My head."

"If you carry nothing but pebbles through the mountains, you *are* sick in the head. Where were you going?"

"To find a monastery."

"Why do they need common rocks?"

"My father was a craftsman. He used rocks."

There is a long pause. Then the little man says, "An ikonographer."

Kostas says nothing. He sees the beard move and knows the little man is smiling.

"So, your father was a criminal too?"

"He was not a criminal."

"That is not what the emperor thinks, boy. That is not what the bishops are saying. Is your father wiser than the emperor and the bishops?"

Kostas stares at the shadowed face of the little man.

The beard moves in the growing light. The man's hand reaches up and lets his hood fall to his shoulders. His nose is missing. Two dark nostrils appear between his eyes and his face is badly misshapen, swollen to one side with a protruding forehead and a tightly sealed eye. The little man grins, a wide smile of broken teeth. "Where did you hide your money?"

"You see already that I have no money."

"You lie. I will beat you till you give me the treasure you have hidden among those scattered stones."

"I have no money. I was carrying enough food to get me into these mountains." Kostas tries to rise but sits down abruptly with the blinding pain in his head. A fresh breeze moves the nearby bushes. He wraps his skinny arms around his chest to control his shivering.

"You do not comment on my strange head, my shortish nose?" says the little man.

"A man is more than a face."

"Oh, I was handsome once as you are now. The emperor's father, Leo, passed those merciful laws that allow thieves to be beaten and mutilated rather than executed."

The boy sits in the dirt and gravel of the trail and watches the man, his heart thumping, his head aching, feeling his helplessness.

"When our last ewe sickened and died," says the little man, "I walked many miles over the mountain to steal another. Without her we would have no lambs in the spring. But the ewe I took had a strange spot beneath a hind leg, and the boy who had kept her recognized her face in our flock and told the officers about the spot under her leg. My father had no money to pay off the men who came. He gave me up to the officers, who broke my head and cheek and jaw and confiscated my nose. Of course, they took half our flock also. So now you see I am marked as a criminal. Such are the mercies of Christian kings."

There is the sharp call of a mountain jay, and the little man jumps suddenly to his feet, steps over, and swings his staff hard.

Kostas jerks back but the staff smashes his nose and the blood is everywhere.

The man steps back and grins. "Foolish little idolator. I could kill you and do the emperor a favor. But I like your new look. Your forehead. Your very flat nose. Now you look like me."

The little man stoops and picks up the bundle of Kostas' clothes and sandals, turns and slips through the crevice in the rock wall, and disappears.

The boy lies back down on the trail on his back, breathing through his mouth, clasping his ribs, and staring at the pale morning sky.

+ + +

When the sun appears above the eastern mountain, he sits up to receive its warmth. Two ravens croak and rise flapping from the gravel of the shadowy streambed below the trail. He glances over and sees his old, frayed bag lying empty on a bush near the stream where the thief must have thrown it. He crawls down to the flowing stream. He drinks, washes the blood from his face and chest and arms, then drinks again. He dips his face in the cold current and lets the blood run from his broken nose, then sits up and breathes. The stench is strong. Beneath the willow bushes he notices the clustered bag that holds the glassed smalti and his mother's ruby necklace. Beyond the bushes on the dry gravel near the stream he sees the stinking skull and ribs of a man long dead. The jackals and ravens have consumed all but the dried rind of flesh on the bones.

He lifts his father's old robe and drops the pebble-covered leather bag into one of the ragged robe's old pockets, then stands up slowly, holding his head. He wraps the old robe around his shoulders and returns to the path and sits down in sunlight, waiting for warmth to return to his skinny bones.

The blood clots again in his nose, and he begins breathing through his mouth. After some time, he considers the several hundred polished stones scattered about the trail.

✛ ✛ ✛

One day, after morning prayers, the fat monk Barnabos leads him back down the ridgeline trail. The forest falls away on the left side of the ridge, occasionally exposing the mountain stream far below, a still ribbon of green and white. They stop and turn into a grove of oaks and retrieve the boy's bag from a hollow between the trunk of an old oak and a boulder. "Since you have now, after these weeks, refused the teachings of our abbot, he tells me you cannot live any longer in one of our cells. He has been patient, Kostas. A full month he let you live with us."

Kostas lifts the bag and swings it to his back. "How far to the next monastery?"

"No. You must not leave. Abbot Tomas is not a cruel man. He even likes you and your argumentative mouth. You may eat with us and attend the prayers, but he will not permit you to speak your beliefs with the brothers. He knows that most of them agree with you and fears this will cause division. And, of course, he will not allow you to use your rock collection."

"But I must work."

"I know a place where you can work. To practice your craft."

"A place?"

"A cave. But Abbot Tomas must not know of the work you do. He has only been here for three years. Many of us believe your work is most worthy. We miss the old images that were torn from our walls. The church council the emperor called to condemn ikons did not include the patriarchs of Jerusalem, Alexandria, and Rome. It was not a valid council. It cannot change the beliefs of so many centuries. But our abbot is young, and the emperor sends us gold coins every year on the Feast of the Magi because he depends on Abbot Tomas to spread his view even in these mountains of the Lebanon."

The boy nods.

"Do not think evil of our abbot, young Kostas. He is a true believer. He has already antagonized the local Muslim officials by preaching openly that the Muslims are heretics. They like the taxes we pay them, but they will not look kindly on this abbot preaching against them. Abbot Tomas came to us from Constantinople and is suspected of being a spy for the emperor."

They walk into sunlight along a flat table of rock that juts over the steep, narrow valley. Far below, the stream washes the feet of the tall cliff of limestone on which they stand.

"You see this little goat track to the side of the great ledge, there, beside that great rock that pushes out to the east?"

Kostas nods.

"There is a cave beneath that great stone where you may live.

I have brought you blankets. Abbot Tomas will not prevent you from attending the liturgies. Perhaps we can feed you if you will do work for the monastery."

✦ ✦ ✦

They sit in afternoon sunlight near the arched stone gate beneath the pines. The old monk points to a tall boulder just beyond the grove of pines. "That old rock. You see it? The brothers call it the bear."

Kostas looks.

"I was a stone carver before my wife died and I became a monk. I told our last abbot I had the power to change a bear into a man." Barnabos smiles. "That bear into St. Maroun so that we would always remember our patron. He told me to get to work, and I did start. You see the chisel work?"

Kostas nods. "It still looks more like a bear than a saint."

"Ah! I had no time, little brother. They kept sending me to the village for supplies or carrying messages. Always something else to do. You would think there would be peace and rest in a monastery. But then our good abbot died, and now Abbot Tomas rejects the shaping of statues. Also, Abbot Tomas needed a treasurer, an old monk whom the brothers would trust. So now I keep the records of our coins and the gifts from the villages. Since I am old, he has relieved me of the donkey trips and lets me sit here as the gate watchman."

Kostas lifts the small bag of coins Barnabos has given him.

"Take the donkeys," the old monk says, "and bring us as many skins of wine as that will buy us in the village. We are growing our own vines now, but it will be many months before we begin to make wine."

Kostas nods. "May I buy a bag of mortar powder?"

"You have already used the last bag?"

Kostas nods. "I found the fine sand I need at the foot of the great waterfall near the village. I bring it back with the mortar. Last month, I walked down to the coast at Tyre. There I found well-made smalti of crimson and shades of blue. They sell cheaply now, Brother Barnabos, for here in Muslim lands there is no market for the making of images, and they cannot be sold in Byzantium."

"And you must have these colored smalti to do your work?"

"In all my travels for the monastery, I have found no rocks of crimson or of the richer shades of blue."

"I will come to the cave to examine your work. Perhaps we can find money for these purchases." The old man sighs. "My hands itch to work again. My hands start swinging the mallet and pushing the chisel and shaping the rock in my head as I sit here keeping watch at the gate."

"The opening of the cave needs to be wider," Kostas says. "You could carve benches on either side."

"Then who would watch this gate?"

"No one comes. Why must you watch?"

"The old man smiles. "Times are difficult. The Muslims have warned Abbot Tomas to stop his preaching against them . . . But yes, buy more mortar."

+ + +

A grey day. Kostas has a fire burning on the narrow ledge just outside the cave. Ten meters above this narrow ledge, the great overhanging ledge of rock projects another two meters. Inside the cave where he works, he has positioned five olive-oil lamps on the cave floor to burn, casting a little light on the ikon. He stirs the pot of mortar and takes a flat, straight-edged rock, scrapes out some mortar, and slaps it onto the stone wall, smoothing it to match the section just below. He has already laid out the necessary stones on a large flat stone lying on the cave floor, small stones of several shades of tan, stones he calls "baked bread and dough" that will shape the ikon's raised hand. He has spent several days choosing the colors and grinding the edges and laying them out so that each one fits tightly to the surrounding pieces, the lines of the finger joints formed by the intersections of rocks: two fingers and a thumb raised, the last two fingers curved, a small hole left vacant in the palm of the hand. All of this he has laid out on a large flat stone so that when the mortar is applied to the cave wall, he can quickly push the stones into the mortar before it begins to harden. With no one to help, it is difficult work. Many times, he has held up his own hand in the nearest lamplight as a model for the larger hand of the ikon. Countless times, he has taken a stone to the mouth of the cave to reexamine the color in the day's natural light. Every clear morning, he awakens in time to watch the partial ikon reflect the morning sun that finds a direct path into the cave for less than an hour. After the sun's revelation, he has sometimes torn out the last day's work, once an entire rainy week's work, to replace the stones with truer colors. Sometimes he chips out a single stone and replaces it. But now he has learned to lay out each arrangement of stones on the flat rock first; then he quickly begins applying each in its place on the wall.

+ + +

In the early morning darkness, he rolls out of his blankets near the back of the cave and moves to the cave's mouth. He stirs the ashes of last evening's fire and finds live embers. He takes a wad of dried grass he keeps in the cave to rekindle the fire and places the grass on the exposed coals. Then he takes the flat mortar rock to fan it into flames, dropping small sticks, then larger ones on the growing fire. He reaches into a wicker basket and takes a piece of the flat bread from the monastery and sits near the fire eating slowly.

He warms his hands as the fire burns low. Soon the sun breaks through a cleft in the eastern mountains, and he turns to look at the ikon. He examines it carefully: the solemn, bearded face is at last complete: the flashing eyes, the firm, serious mouth, and the hand raised in blessing with the missing piece in the palm.

He takes a ceramic cup in which he mixes a small amount of sandy mortar with water, walks back to the ikon, removes the mortar with his thumb, and pushes it into the hole in the hand. Then he reaches behind his neck and unclasps the golden necklace he has been wearing for the last week. With his two thumbs, he forces the ruby from its gold ring, wipes it with a cloth, then pushes the ruby into the wounded hand.

He stands back to see the red sunlight burning within the hand.

✦ ✦ ✦

He has sent her letters as often as he could find someone in the village who was traveling north and west through Ephesus. Twice last year, he sent her letters. He has not found a carrier through the winter months but hopes the village coppersmith will again make his annual journey to Ephesus to make his sales and purchases once the weather breaks. Only Kostas' mother knows of his work—she and Brother Barnabos. He uses his father's names for stones to inform her, but he never makes any obvious mention of what he is doing in the letters lest the person entrusted with the letter find someone who can read it. In his last letter, he wrote, "I have woven Tyrian reds for the left shoulder with a fabric of Damascus and Antioch wines. Athenian sparkles on the sleeves with linen folds of bread dough and August grass and baked bread in their places." Anyone reading the letter might think him an eccentric weaver of fabrics and clothing or an even more eccentric cook.

She has sent letters in return. She is well. She has learned again to love her life and wishes the same for him. She promises her prayers. She wishes she could come to visit, but old Demetrius cannot travel.

The next day, he walks up to the monastery and asks Brother Jonas for ink and quill to write a letter about the placing of the ruby. He writes: "My father's heart of fire and my mother's wounded heart have found a home in the Maker's hand."

✦ ✦ ✦

Sunday morning. Late winter. A frost on the trailside grasses as Kostas climbs the old path to the monastery for the morning liturgy and the meal to follow. He stops and glances up the trail. Three goats scramble through the arched gateway. He steps aside as they rush past him and leap off into the forest. He sees a haze hanging in the pine trees ahead and wonders why a fog would now be drifting over the mountains. Then he smells smoke.

He hurries up the trail and through the wall's stone arch. And stops. Down the meadow, beside the leafless branches of the pondside willows, he sees twenty horses. A young man stands near the horses holding a lance. Horses of the Muslim militia. All is quiet but for the crackling of fire along one side of the monastery roof and a strange, regular slapping sound.

A bulky grey figure comes hobbling through the smoke that is drifting along the side wall of the monastery. The man has a bundle over his shoulder, and he is coughing through the smoke toward the front gate. It is old Barnabos, staggering toward the stone wall.

Kostas hurries to meet his friend, takes the sack, hoists it over his shoulder, and asks, "What is this? Where are we taking it?"

Barnabos stares at him for a moment, gasping for air, then motions Kostas to follow him into the forest.

They make their way down the trail and into the forest to the old oak and boulder with the hollow beneath, where years before Kostas had hidden his bag of rocks.

"Come again this night," pants the old man. "Then take this sack to your cave. Keep it there. You must never return it to the monastery!"

"What is it?"

"The king's gold he has sent these many years to Abbot Tomas."

"But I cannot! I must not . . ."

"Silence! Hear me. We will rebuild the roof of the monastery, but the Muslims must never know that there was gold here." The old man holds his panting chest, draws a deep breath, and coughs. "Ah! I am too old for this."

Kostas opens the sack and looks down at heavy gold coins.

"They burn the monastery to punish Abbot Tomas for his preaching against Islam. They are beating him now with a flat stick in front of all the brothers, but they are merciful; they will not execute him. Not this time. But Kostas!" He turns his heavy face and long grey beard toward the young man and stares fiercely into his eyes. "If they find this great treasure, they will not only take it all, but then the soldiers, with or without orders, will return to steal again. They think now that we are a poor monastery far up in the mountains with nothing but a few goats. If they know the emperor sends us riches, they will return again and again, and perhaps they will slay us all so that we will not accuse them of robbing a holy place."

"Perhaps," Kostas says, "I can use the coins to buy supplies for you."

"Ah! No! Are you beyond all knowledge? If you, this poor donkey boy, appears with gold in his hand, they will know it is the monastery's gold."

"But I can say you have sent it to buy supplies from the village."

"The Muslims have taken the little money we had. I had hidden this sack beneath the floor because we never use the heavy coins. Abbot Tomas believes we must live by our own labor and the gifts of the mountain people. He does not know what to do with this. He once traveled to Tyre to buy cloth and vestments and two beautiful candlesticks, but that is all. And if you appear with gold coins in the villages, the militia will know they missed something. You know this. The people of the mountains, even visitors from afar, give us a few coins, or cloth, or barley, or cheese and fruits, but not heavy gold pieces. One of these coins spent, and the news will spread fire through these mountains."

"What then?"

"Are you not an ikonographer?"

"What?"

"Use this gold to crown the Christ you have been forming for these three years. Create a work of great beauty, boy. Give our king a crown, a crown of blazing gold! Let the gold shine forth from the face of the Holy One. He is worthy of this!"

"And never return it to the monastery?"

"It will be a work done in great silence. A gift to God. The soldiers may well return and burn us again, for I doubt if our abbot will stop his preaching. He will in time be forced to return to Constantinople, but this poor monastery must never become rich in gold. And now the abbot will believe the Muslims have taken this sack. He will be relieved of this burden."

"You will not confess this taking of the gold? It is a great sin."

"Ah! It is not mine. It is not yours. You must never allow this to become yours. It will be a great temptation for a poor boy like you, a powerful desire for anyone who finds it. Give it all to God, boy. Give it all. Make it beautiful. Make it glorious! I will help you. Tell no one. I will come to you and begin work on the benches and steps. I am old. I cannot help rebuild our monastery roof, so I will ask Abbot Tomas for permission to retreat to a cave, to become a hermit like the desert Egyptians. I am useless as a gate watchman. Every day I fall asleep. And the crown, Kostas. Or better, the halo, make it a halo, will catch the eastern sun in the mornings. The Holy One will shine! It must be done." With that old Barnabos hobbles away through the trees and climbs the trail into smoke.

✛ ✛ ✛

"Already, one bench is roughed in, Brother Kostas!" The old monk is on his knees at the mouth of the cave. He places his mallet and chisel on the floor, then leans over and sweeps the rubble from the surface of the bench with his forearm, sits back on his heels, and claps his big hands, sending up a puff of dust.

"My hands ache, young Kostas; my back pains me, but how I love this work! Even in the heat of summer. After all these years, to form stone again. Even a simple bench. To see in my mind the shape and to slowly, stroke by stroke, bring it to life."

Kostas is pouring a little olive oil into one of the clay dish lamps on the floor of the cave. He then picks up each lamp and places it on one of seven small rock shelves Barnabos has cut into the walls. Then he takes a stick from the fire and lights each wick. He looks up. "Bring the stone to life you say? Will this bench of rock someday speak to you? Will you have a conversation?"

Barnabos frowns, then remembers. "Do not mock our abbot, Kostas. Perhaps he spoke unwisely that day to a young boy, but he has given you work all these years."

"You are right, brother. I am grateful. Very grateful." Kostas takes the ceramic pot of oil to the storage area on the far side of the cave, then turns to observe how the light of evening is enhanced by the flames that illumine the face and flicker from the twelve planks of gold that spread into the solid halo behind the head of the great mosaic.

+ + +

"You still have no woman?"

They sit at the lip of the cave on a late winter morning, their legs and bare feet crossed beneath their robes, a small fire of sticks and pinecones burning on the ledge between them, the smoke twisting away in a dawn breeze. Ten meters below them, the roots of a twisted apple tree grip a stone ledge, its trunk and bare limbs rise toward them, the twigs of the highest branches moving in the occasional breeze and gently scratching the cliff stones near them. Below the tree, the cliff drops—a sheer fall to the mountain stream, so far that the white water of the rapids and the surge of current are a still, silent image, though actually full of movement and life.

Old Barnabos shrugs his right shoulder. "My shoulder aches, young Kostas. Our stone benches are even harder to sleep on than the dirt floors of the monastery cells."

"I am no longer young, Brother Barnabos."

"True, true. Most definitely true. It has been ten years since you walked naked into my life. And you still have no woman?"

"I have a friend."

"A woman friend?" The old man looks up from the fire and grins broadly. "You have not told old Brother Barnabos of this?"

"She likes me. Her father, too, likes me."

"Who, who, who?" He holds his palms to the fire.

"You know Daphne, one of the daughters of Mustafa, the coppersmith down in the village?"

"Mustafa is Muslim! How can you think of marriage?"

"Her mother is a Greek slave. He even gave his daughter a Greek name, and he allows his daughter and her mother to attend the liturgies in the village church near the great waterfall."

Barnabos pulls at his beard. "Her father will allow this? A Greek boy for his daughter?"

"He is not particularly religious. He wants to appease his Christian customers. And our ikon here is finished, even the benches. I have more time now for her father. He likes to talk. I spend hours listening to his stories."

"So you can observe his daughter?"

"There are worse reasons to talk to an old gossip. He taps away at his copper plates and tells me the news. He was the one who first told me what they did to Abbot Tomas."

"Ah! A terrible thing. Brother Mathias said the soldiers laughed when they sliced out his tongue. He almost choked to death on his own blood."

They sit for a time in silence looking out across the steep valley to the mountains beyond. In the night, a light snow has whitened the peaks and powdered the firs and cedars and pines. In the dawn light, a breeze sometimes sends the falling flakes up and about the side of the precipice, then releases them to settle upon the pines below.

Kostas adds a few sticks to their fire.

Barnabos breaks the silence. "I never get to the village. How old is this girl?"

"Younger than me."

"And you are what, 25 years? Is this now serious?"

"Yes."

"Have you told her of your work in the cave?"

"I cannot."

"Cannot? She thinks you are only the donkey boy for the monastery?"

"I call it 'master of supplies.' And old Mustafa wants to hire me to fetch his goods from Ephesus. This spring, I hope to visit my mother after all these years."

Barnabos smiles and nods his bare head. "This is wonderful news, my boy. Your mother knows of the ikon, you said."

"Yes. These ten years. But she is too old to travel. She is pleased that I am fulfilling my vocation."

"That you are. That you are. But ah! Surely one day, boy, you will, perhaps, give this young woman your great secret, and when you are married and can trust her, you will bring her here to pray. She will be dazzled, Kostas! Walking in a dream to know her donkey boy is a holy writer!"

"No."

"No? She must see what a splendid craftsman you have become!"

"You tempt me, brother. No one must destroy this image after all the years we have worked on it. You know that even an accidental slip of her tongue, pride in her new husband, the need to defend me to her family for they know me only as a donkey boy, any of this, and the holy ikon would be lost."

The old monk holds his hands to the fire, then rubs the warmth into his cheeks. A cold breeze whirls snow along the ledge. Barnabos reaches for his head cloth and winds it deftly around his bald head and fastens it. "Of course. Of course. But what a pity, my boy, what a pity that no one can know, not even a wife!"

"Yes. You told me to make it a gift to God. And so it is. He sees."

The old monk leans into the cave and reaches for a basket of dried apples. He hands a shriveled apple to Kostas and takes one himself. He points east. "You see, my boy, the sun is about to break over the mountains."

They sit in silence eating the fruit, spitting the seeds over the cliff. "We will soon have a new abbot, Kostas. Abbot Tomas has healed now, but it was terrible, terrible to see such an eloquent speaker, such a persuasive preacher silenced in this way."

Kostas nods. "How is he dealing with this?"

"What can an abbot do who has no tongue?"

"He can write words. Instruct through writing."

"He will not write. Perhaps this is your doing."

Kostas looks up. "Mine? How?"

Barnabos holds his hands over the small fire. "That first morning."

"Ten years ago?"

"Yes. You said something about words being symbolic, like ikons."

"He remembers this?"

"A thorn in his mind, a thorn to his brain. He spoke to me of this many times. Said that what 'the little theologian,' as he called you, said was true, that the words of men are but the symbols of foolish men, not the revelations of the Creator. They are nothing, he says, but the interpretations of small minds. And that our many words dilute the power of the sacred Scriptures."

"You agree?"

"Well, of course I see that words are symbols, as you saw as a boy. But surely, I told him, God gives wisdom to men. To help us apply the holy Scriptures to our daily work without watering truth. 'Watered wine! Watered wine!' he would cry."

"Even watered wine can be refreshing," says Kostas.

"Abbot Tomas thinks not. For years he has wrestled with this. More and more, he has spoken less and less. He would let one of the brothers read us the Holy Scriptures, then he would say, "So it is written, so let it be done." Then he would sit down. No interpretation. No homily. We sit and wait. Sit and think till the liturgy of the sacrament begins."

"The brothers accept this?" Kostas asks.

"Not well, not well. Everyone wants their abbot to apply

the text to our lives, to use wise words, words of comfort, even words of rebuke when necessary."

"Why, then, if he rarely speaks, did the Muslims cut out his tongue?"

"Ah! In the villages, he would recite what he calls the pure words of the apostles, speaking out boldly in the market. Standing on a rock, he would cry out the words of Saint Paul or Saint Peter, but he refused to offer arguments to the Muslims in debate. You see, Kostas, he is no coward. He is a true believer, even if he mistrusts even Holy Church to interpret the faith."

The fire crackles and spits sparks that float out over the cliff. The far mountainside fades in the falling snow for a few minutes, but the cloud passes, opening the skies beyond the silhouetted mountains to the east. The canopy of fir trees below has gathered a light covering of snow.

They finish eating the apples and spit the seeds over the cliff. Slowly, the sun breaks free of the eastern mountain. They sit silently, there on the side of the cliff, looking down at the stream, the sun on their faces.

"But he's a hard, hard believer, Kostas. He hates the monasteries that hold to the old ways. He used to say that traditions are nothing but ashes made of good wood, though a visiting monk once responded by saying traditions are a fire that illuminates by burning good wood. Abbot Tomas was not pleased, though he did not rebuke the monk."

"He never visits his old treasurer here in the cave," Kostas remarks.

"I told him it was a hard cave to find, which is true, and he was always too busy to track old Barnabos to his lair. Still, he is a good man, Kostas. Perhaps a saint."

"We must watch behind us," says Kostas, "when we leave the monastery after prayers and meals. He must not find us here."

Barnabos rubs his knuckles and kneads the muscles of a hand. "I am glad our work is done, Kostas. I finished the three steps into the cave. Still, I have work to do leveling the floor. But one day, when it is time, the brothers will elect a new abbot, and perhaps this abbot will approve of ikons. Perhaps then we will be able to share this with the brotherhood and people from the village may come here to pray."

"But Brother Barnabos, they will see the gold. The word will fly on every wind if word ever leaks of our gold halo. Thieves will appear in the night and tear it all out. Perhaps the militia will return. You know this. All the work of melting the gold, pouring it into your molds, polishing it to perfection, all will be lost."

Barnabos moans and nods. "Yes. Yes. Yes. What a pity. A pity. Ah! What a pity."

"It can wait, Barnabos. It is our gift to God, as you first told me. And the floor can wait too; let your old hands heal. We can work on it this spring."

"I look forward to meeting this woman you have found, my friend. This Daphne. I recall her as a little girl when I used to visit Mustafa." Barnabos pulls at his long beard, twisting it around a thick finger. "But it is a pity. A great pity that the brothers cannot worship here. That the village cannot share in this treasure. That they cannot look upon the holy face. That your own wife . . ."

"It is too rich. The day someone finds it is the day it is torn from us."

"Ah! This hurts my very soul." The old man pulls at his beard. "The thought that such an image could ever die . . .

Look! The light will be upon the ikon now!"

They turn toward the interior of the cave, and Barnabos pushes himself heavily to his feet and steps down the carved steps into the cave with Kostas following. Barnabos sits down on the blankets that lie on his chiseled bench on the right side and Kostas sits down on the blankets on the left-hand bench to allow the sunlight passage. Barnabos begins the Friday morning psalm, chanting:

"O Lord, I have heard of your renown,
And feared, O Lord, your work. . ."

and Kostas turns his eyes to the great ikon he has so carefully and painstakingly worked over the years, each stone ground down to fit with the next, with added squares of deep blue smalti inserted beyond the rays of solid gold that emanate from behind the strong face of the King, with shades of red and crimson flowing down from a shoulder.

"In the course of the years revive it,"
and Kostas joins in the repetition:
"In the course of the years make it known;
In your wrath remember compassion."
They pause and take up the second verse:
"God comes from Teman,
The Holy One from Mount Paran,
Covered are the heavens with His glory,
And with His praise the earth is filled."
They pause, and begin again:
"His splendor spreads like the light . . ."
When they finish the psalm, they sit in silence, gazing upon the ikon at the back of the cave. That bearded face so powerful in the sudden light, a ruby-red glimmer in the wound of the

hand raised in blessing, the twelve gold rays blazing around the face of a man like the sun, a blinding light that closes their eyes.

✦ ✦ ✦

It was a long time ago. Months passed into years and years into decades. The apple tree went down in a storm, its roots ripped from the rock, its limbs broken away and scattered down the cliff, catching here and there then weathering smooth and hard. The winds wore the wood away decade after decade till the broken limbs were no more than wet splinters and pockets of black soil in the cliff crevices. From spit seeds, new trees rose from the rock ledges, drank the rain and snow, bore their fruit, and in time broke away. Below, forests burned and grew again. Above, the monastery fell into disrepair, abandoned at last by three old monks walking down the ridge with sacks on their shoulders.

✦ ✦ ✦

They had heard the sound, the old man and the young. A rattling of stones beside the heavy ledge of stone that protruded from the high cliff over the cave. They had both stood up in alarm from the benches and faced the sunlight as a figure broke the brightness. They could not see who it was till Abbot Tomas rushed past them with a strangled cry and began clawing at the great ikon.

The old man and the young had stood there shocked as the abbot picked up one of Barnabos' chisels and began stabbing it into the ikon's regal face.

The old man had been quicker than the young. Had slammed into the outraged abbot and jerked him away from the ikon and into the young man. The heavy old man had placed all his weight behind the gabbling, shouting, wordless abbot and the stumbling, sobbing young man and had shoved with all his might, but the abbot was strong and quick. He ducked and wrenched himself away from the old monk's arms. The abbot then turned quickly and shoved Barnabos and the boy toward the mouth of the cave. The two, Kostas and Barnabos, stumbled backwards up the three steps, their momentum carrying them over the lip of the cliff.

Their bodies snapped through the grey limbs of the apple tree and rolled as one into empty space, each man clutching the other. Dropping, dropping in a rapid rolling flutter of robes and bare feet.

+ + +

Abbot Tomas leapt up the steps and fell to his knees at the edge of the precipice panting. He stared down through the leafless broken limbs of the old apple tree in disbelief. Far below the winter stream flowed on. The tall pines and fir trees stood. The slight dusting of snow on the canopy had darkened where the two had crashed through the limbs and onto the frozen rocks.

Tomas grasped the rocks at the cliff edge and stared, a stiff frozen figure in a grey robe.

Slowly, slowly, he turned toward the cave and crawled toward the threshold of the cave. Sunlight still poured through the cave opening, illuminating the majestic figure that faced him.

He raised his eyes to the ikon.

He panted and stared. His breath began coming in gasps. At last he tried to say, "I have killed my own sons," though he could not tongue the words. "I have killed your brothers!" He squinted and blinked for a moment at the bright reflection of sunlight emanating from the gold halo, then he dropped his gaze to the floor of the cave and crumpled slowly forward, his forehead finding the cold stone threshold that old Barnabos had spent hours and hours leveling and smoothing. The abbot's long grey hair spread across the entry.

His body began convulsing with sobs. He tried to murmur a confession, but his garbled voice would speak nothing but vowels that broke into a high wail. He remained thus till the sun passed on, leaving the cave in quiet shadow.

There he knelt through the long day and into the longest night. There he stayed through much of the following day, his mind a blank tablet of stone till at last his crumpled body fell into sleep on the cave floor.

He awoke shivering in the early morning. He forced himself to his feet and stepped stiffly into the dark cave. He found the lamps on their carved shelves but had no way to light them.

He left the cave and made his way up the goat track to the monastery. He walked in among the monks who were moving about the building on a winter morning, attending to their chores. They were used to seeing the wordless abbot and bowed as he passed.

He went to a burning lamp, lifted it, and carried it back to the cave, where he lit Kostas' seven lamps.

✦ ✦ ✦

He lived the rest of his days in the cave, coming to the monastery for the liturgies and for simple meals, but always returning to the image of the one whose face had long ago received him.

+ + +

Monks followed him to the cave. He spoke not a word, but simply pointed them to the ikon, then knelt and prayed. The monks were, of course, shocked, but eventually began joining him in his prayers. Two of the monks came to live with him, caring for him and each other, sitting for long hours on the lip of the cliff, commenting on the beauty of the valley and mountains, discussing theology, repeating the Psalms morning, noon, and evening.

One day the abbot joined them on the lip of the cliff, a place he had so studiously avoided that the monks presumed he was afraid of heights. He sat down there and let his feet hang over the cliff. He then forced his gaze down to the living trees below where the stream flowed. Tears came to his eyes. He stayed there all that night as a sickle moon cut its way slowly across a star-filled sky.

In the morning he joined the two for the recitation of prayers and psalms. For the first time he sang with them. No words, but the melody and cadences of the chants accompanied their words, and the two monks were pleased. A great sadness had lifted.

+ + +

In the fall of the year 787, hundreds of bishops gathered again in the Byzantine city of Nicaea for a great council, the Second Council of Nicaea. There, with representatives of the great patriarchates, they made a declaration reinstating the use of ikons and other images and decorations. Ikons of Christ, the Holy Virgin, saints, and martyrs could again, as the Council document states, be "exhibited on

the walls of churches, in the homes, and in all conspicuous
places, by the roadside and everywhere . . . for the more they
are contemplated, the more they move to fervent memory."

✦ ✦ ✦

And the centuries walked on. Bushes and vines grew up over
the face of the cave, their flowers calling the bees of spring, their
leaves bringing the summer spider webs, fall winds drying and
dropping the leaves.

One winter, part of the heavy protruding ledge above the
opening broke away and crashed through the apple trees into the
forest below, sending great bounding rocks smashing into the
stream where they caught the current that swirled into turbulent
pools and surged into whitewater rapids.

The first millennium hobbled slowly away. The boulders in
the stream broke into stones, and some eventually wore away
into flat pebbles. Again and again on the high ledge, apple trees
rose into the wind and the sun, dropping the flowers of spring,
dropping the fruits of fall into the forest below.

Mice made nests in the recesses of the cave, and always
the crickets found safety in the dead leaves at the opening and
chirped their evening psalms while quiet bats flitted in and out
like strangez airborne monks. Jackals found the dark cave and
made it a refuge for their young, feeding on the mice and leaving
those delicate bones scattered in clumps across the rough floor.

Each day received the sunlight and each night gave it away
again as the centuries walked away, accepting the passing of feet
on the trails above and the cutting of timber below.

One day, men and women came up the valley and planted
orchards in the cut forest along the stream and added olive and

almond and fig trees that fed the bees and welcomed the birds while the men built homes of wood and clay and stone and laid themselves down to rest each night.

In time, the earth took them in and then waited on their children and grandchildren, giving to them its fruits and grains and to their sheep, grasses, and to their goats, shrubs and thorns. And the seasons turned and turned again, moving quietly down the river of the years.

Wars broke the people. Faction savaged faction. Heavily armored crusaders from distant lands pounded down the coast on their huge, snorting, European warhorses, and men built high, elaborate stone forts, and the Muslims in their thousands upon thousands fought back with their scimitars and bows and light cavalry, and men killed, and horses fled this way and that, and children and women hid in the forests, and the land received each one in its turn as the "unstilled world still whirled."

Fugitives came again to their burned homes, and wounded men limped back from the wars to plan and plant and prune, and young boys again found their scattered flocks and followed them up the valley and sat in quiet sunlight or shade playing reed flutes and returned evenings to the little sheep pens. And the young girls rose with the dawn and helped their mothers make the bread and ate with their families then played along the banks of the beautiful stream and on warm afternoons washed clothes in the cold waters and in the evenings received their meals of barley bread and pine nuts, chickpeas and almonds and perhaps on feast days a lamb, and in time they too raised children, grew old, and returned to the good earth.

The high cliff was appreciated as a buffer against the north winds, a shelter for the orchards. Only on a rare winter day might a young girl or boy watching the flight of a hawk or the swift rise of a falcon look up and notice a small dark opening behind vines and shrubs high up the cliff beneath a broken ledge. And the centuries plodded on and on.

+ + +

Came a day when great machines roared through the skies and heavy tubes on wheeled conveyances spit fire and smoke and thunder and blasted homes to rubble. Across the world, nations battled nations, and factions tore at factions, and machines breathing smoke and coughing out steel rattled up and down tarred gravel roads and ripped through orchards and fields of grain, and the second millennium rumbled toward its violent end.

+ + +

Waited the wordless word at the back of the cave. In winter, the morning light would sometimes break through the leafless bushes and vines to find the great image spattered with guano and veiled in dust. Waiting still. Lifting a wounded hand.

MOSAIC

Down the valley, clouds beyond clouds were congregating their power, muttering and bickering as if the old Phoenician storm gods were plotting destruction upon the occasional villages perched along the ridges of this steep valley of Lebanon. Seated on a limestone ledge above the valley, Yusuf watched the stream far below him, but he was too far up to see the rush and fall of its current. White rapids stood still; clear green currents lay fixed like glass.

A sudden gust of wind. He pulled his stocking cap down over his forehead and turned again to watch the man, maybe a mile away, hiking up the mountain trail.

Yusuf himself had chosen to come that way five years before, climbing the old trail on foot so that he could take in the valley and mountains of his youth, each turn of the path opening an old memory. The footpath was unforgiving: shale to slip on, fallen rocks and roots to step over, limbs to duck under, a sheer cliff falling away on the right, and always the trail twisting upward with hard ascents, quick declines, tough going all the way.

Yusuf was now fifty-four, but even five years before it had been a difficult climb. He remembered stopping to sit on this very limestone ledge that bright spring morning, gazing south down the valley where little rectangles of flowering apple and almond trees alternated with patches of olive trees, where dirt roads and footpaths interlaced small plots of plowed earth, all of that patchwork mosaic along the valley floor underlined by the winding course of Wadi Jezzine, flowing blue and green in the sunlight. A welcoming sight after the loneliness of East Dearborn, Michigan, the largely Arab suburb of metropolitan Detroit where he had lived for thirty-five years, managing four car washes. Not a lucrative job, but a stable one; Ford and GM factories had foundered in 2008, but Detroiters still loved their cars enough to keep them clean.

He glanced back at the distant climber. He must be a stranger to these mountains; no one but goatherds used that trail anymore, and the climber was obviously a novice: clambering, stumbling, resting, moving on, hunched over beneath a backpack—a small black beetle scrabbling and slipping over gravel and dirt.

Yusuf put a cigarette to his lips. The little Melkite village of his youth, and now of his late middle age, lay beyond the climber out of sight. Behind Yusuf, a terrace of apple trees was white with spring, the black limbs swaying and rattling in the sudden gusts that whipped white flowers into the air and sent them swirling over the cliff. His clippers and pruning shears lay beside him; he had spent the morning cutting out the dead limbs of winter, and he now felt the strain and ache. With one hand he massaged the ropy muscles of his forearm and turned to face the storm.

The Lebanese Civil War that had broken out in 1975, and the sudden Israeli invasion that followed in 1982, with the southern Lebanese Christian militia allying itself for a time with Israel, had smashed his family and driven him as a boy to America.

He was fourteen the morning they fled the fighting. Shaken by the roar of low-flying Israeli jets, he had gripped his mother's hand, half pulling her along, fleeing their village, looking for a cave of refuge his father had described, leaving the chaos of militia factions scrambling into lines of defense. His father and older brother had hurried down the ridgeline to help defend the larger city, Jezzine, while his father had given him, fourteen years old, the responsibility of guiding his mother to safety in the cave.

Then, just beyond one of his family's olive groves, a sudden staccato burst of an automatic weapon. His mother had gasped and jerked him into the dirt, not crying out, not saying a word. He had lost hold of her hand and looked back to see her collapsed on the trail holding her mouth. Her startled eyes found him, and her bloodied hand reached out. Shot in the mouth, her blood running through broken teeth, her voice gone.

She had died in the village six days later, never able to speak a word, breathing with difficulty, unable to swallow food.

On the last morning, his father had pulled him from the bed he shared with his older brother. Yusuf remembered hearing a dog bark somewhere outside the house. The dusty slant of sunlight through a window. The smell of disinfectant as he followed his father to his mother's bed. His brother was gone with the militia, but his mother's eyes were waiting for him, the gauze wrapping around her neck, the blood-soaked bandages below her jaw, her lips and cheek badly swollen, but her brown eyes alive, intense. When he came to her bed, she reached out to him and took his face in her calloused hands and stared long into his eyes. He had felt the strength of those eyes. They were filled with a passionate, wordless longing.

In the following months, he had lived with agonizing rage. He told his father again and again that he would take a gun and kill the murderers, but finally his father had grabbed him fiercely by the shoulders and asked him who exactly he would be killing, since he had seen no one on the mountainside that morning when the shot hit, nor anyone in the olive grove. Was it a Fatah militiaman as Yusuf supposed? Christian militia? Israeli commandos? Who could say? "Perhaps," his father said, "it was a frightened fourteen-year-old boy like you!"

But Yusuf's rage had burned on, and he was determined to kill. He was making plans with an older friend to run off and join the Christian militia when his father solved the problem by driving him to Beirut and putting him on a plane to America to work for his uncle Ibrahim in Detroit.

✦ ✦ ✦

Thirty-five years later, his uncle Ibrahim willed Yusuf these apple and almond and olive trees after Yusuf's father died.

The day Yusuf returned to Jezzine, he had walked up the hill to the Melkite Christian churchyard and found the small family gravestones. He had stood there reading the names: his mother Amal's name carved in Arabic, his father's, his brother's.

He had stood there, his own heart a stone.

Jezzine had grown in the last 35 years, but his own village a few miles up the valley was much as he remembered it: homes collected along the mountain ridge quiet in the morning light, but as the day warmed, the people talkative, argumentative, the place alive with the braying of donkeys and roosters, with dogs, cats, chickens, children running and shouting, a few trucks rumbling along the ridgeline road. Not a single car wash.

+ + +

He breathed deeply of the cool breeze and looked back at the climbing beetle. The man would not see him perched here on this heavy outcropping of limestone. An unpracticed eye would glance up and see only the white wash of the blossoming trees on the high bluff. He breathed in the American tobacco and released the smoke to hurry away along the wind.

The man was still moving, climbing steadily, growing larger. He was wearing a baseball cap. A merchant? Some relative arriving from France or England or America? But he had heard of no one expected in the village.

Thunder rumbled up the valley. The sky behind the climber was dark. Far down the valley, the olive and orchard trees patching the valley floor and the sooty pines of the opposite mountain were now fading into rain.

Yusuf sat smoking another cigarette, enjoying the coming storm.

With the first snap of nearby lightning and scattered drops, he picked up his clippers and shears and slipped off the rock shelf, slid to its side, and climbed down the stony channel the storm water would take. He ducked beneath the overhanging ledge of limestone, pulled himself around clinging vines and creepers, stepped along a ledge and then into a square-cut opening ten feet wide. He paused and turned back to watch the opposite mountainside being consumed by wind and rain. The climber would have little protection. He flicked away the stub of his cigarette, bent down, and entered.

Inside, he stepped down three stone steps into the secure silence of the cave, felt his way along the familiar stone bench cut from the right side of the cave wall, where he always sat and put down the shears and clippers. The place was dark, quiet, not large—maybe twenty feet to the back wall and about fifteen feet wide. The floor had been roughly chipped flat long ago, and the ceiling curved up into darkness.

He sat down and leaned back against the cave wall, listening to the storm.

The rain came. Heavy and hard, slashing against the vines and bushes and rocks outside. Lightning hit nearby with a concussion of thunder. Gusts of wind slapped the rain this way and that. He heard the water in the channel he had just descended beginning to rush down past the cave into the cliffside bushes and leap over the precipice. He thought of the climbing beetle, sighed, and closed his eyes. After the storm passed, he would look for the man. He reached into his shirt pocket for his cigarettes but remembered where he was and put his hands between his knees.

He loved the sound of the storm and the muffled silence inside. He could smell the fresh, cold rain—rain that would be good for the apples and almonds if the winds didn't tear the trees apart.

After a few minutes, he reached to the side of the bench and pulled up a bottle of wine, twisted out the cork between thumb and finger, and drank. He set the bottle on the floor beside the bench and reached for the flat pieces of pita he had wrapped in a cloth. He sat there tearing off pieces and chewing slowly.

+ + +

A winter storm in Detroit. Power lines down in the snow. No lights in the apartment complex. No television. No radio. His wife Najwa lit a vanilla-scented candle and placed it on the small dining room table, then returned to the kitchen. The afternoon snow was still falling and his eighteen-year-old daughter Amal, named for his mother (though everyone called her Amy), sat across from him twisting her short black hair around her index finger. She said the boy was moving to Iowa, to Des Moines. Had a track scholarship to Drake University. She would follow him there. Take classes at a community college.

"But we have no money to send you to college in such a faraway place," he said.

"Student loans," she said. She had already talked to the high school counselor. She would pick up a part-time job as a waitress. "I'll do just fine, Papi."

America. Who could hold a daughter to the family in America? He tried to remember her face now: dark eyes, lovely skin, his own straight nose. He remembered the hair. Why so short? She needed long hair to balance his nose. But he could convince her of nothing.

From their upstairs apartment, he watched the falling snow: the black telephone wires sagging beneath the weight of wet snow and sloping away into the drifting white. His wife in the kitchen was heating tea over the blue flames of a little propane camp stove. She opened the lid of the metal teapot and dropped in the tea leaves to soak. She glanced up at her husband. Seeing his troubled eyes, she walked back to the dining room table and moved the scented candle nearer her husband.

He turned his eyes and stared into the flame. He knew his daughter would leave.

"But Papi, you know I'll call. We'll stay close. I'll write. You know Bobby likes you. This won't come between us."

And he knew even then that distances could not be overcome by the poor, that the manager of car washes could not fly to Des Moines nor fly her home.

And then, just six months later, the stroke: his wife crumpled up at the bottom of the stairway with a bag of onions and eggplant and peppers crushed beneath her.

Then the slow recovery in the spring of the following year ending with a grand mal seizure, and he was suddenly alone for the first time in 35 years, and even his daughter's weeklong visit for the funeral could not comfort him. But he had never doubted that life could be harsh. He had seen worse as a young man in these mountains.

Two months after the funeral came Uncle Ibrahim's illness—not unexpected for such an old businessman. He had called Yusuf to his hospital bed.

"Yusuf, my wife Hiba and our son-in-law . . . you've met Freddy, haven't you? . . . will keep running our bakery, but I will sell the car washes." The old man gave him a quick hard glance.

"But Uncle!"

I know, I know, Yusuf. You need the work. But you don't need the work, boy." Yusuf was 49 years old and his uncle still called him boy.

"You are alone now," Ibrahim said.

"Amy is in Iowa with her boyfriend."

"So you are alone. Now don't speak. Listen."

Uncle Ibrahim, his skin thin and dry as faded parchment, his eyes now half blind, told him a strange tale. After he had married in the Melkite church in Jezzine, a rich Byzantine wedding ceremony that Yusuf still remembered, Ibrahim and Yusuf's father had continued to work their father's apple orchards and olive trees north of the village. Once, when Israeli jets screamed over the valley, Ibrahim had ducked under a ledge and found a cave overgrown with bushes and vines. He had torn through the vines and entered the cave. "Your father, did he speak of the cave?"

"What cave?" Yusuf then remembered his father's hurried directions on the day his mother was shot, but they had never made it to the cave.

"A cave you will find. A cave you must find." His uncle looked up at the hospital room ceiling, and Yusuf was surprised by the old man's tears. "I commit crime."

"A crime, Uncle? You have always been a good and honest . . ."

"Don't speak. Listen. Stealing is a crime, no? I many times hoping to leave major problems with civil war by coming to America but have no money then. Hard days. I have two babies to worry those days. When I find cave, I show my brother, your father. He tell me not to do it. Argue again and again. But I tell him we got to get out, go to America, find safe place, start business, support our new families. He tell me we cannot betray this land, this place, our father's land. This God's place, he say, not ours. I say God can afford to loan us a cave. Your father, he say, no, no, no. But I am older brother. I do it. With hammer and chisel. Then I take Hiba and the two girls here to Dearborn."

"Did what with hammer . . ."

The old man flicked his hand impatiently and kept talking. "Later, for you, your father lets me pay your plane ticket to the States. Remember how crazy you were then, boy? After your beautiful mother, Amal, get shot and die and your older brother get caught by the Muslim militia, that is too much for your father. He send you to America, and I buy the car washes so you can work. He know where the money for this purchases come from, but even he look past conscience for you, Yusuf, for you."

The tears followed the crevices along his nose. He blinked and took a hesitant breath. "You fix my crime."

Old Ibrahim's hair was gone. Brown splotches darkened his pale forehead and sunken cheeks. "I promise your father I will pay back. There in Jezzine. Ten years before you come to USA. I give him my word, boy. Do you understand? To your own father my brother."

The cord for a heart monitor ran beneath his hospital gown to a blinking machine. He sniffed once and coughed. "I sell car washes. The state will give good dollars for the one on Mechanics Street. The others in Dearborn and Livonia not bad money too. You know Yitzhak, the old jeweler downtown?"

Yusuf shook his head no.

"He is good craftsman. He will shape this gold I have bought like the old gold. You must know I always believe I will pay back. I take flash Polaroid pictures of each piece and draw lines around all twelve on paper so I can one day repair. And you, Yusuf, will put back these into cave. I deed you the land, the two apple orchards, the almonds, the olive trees. Our family house in the village. All this yours if you fix my old sin. Go back, boy.

Go back to Jezzine. To our village. Take the old trees and make them young again. You do not love this USA as I do. You will pray again at family grave for me, for your wife Najwa, for Amal, for your father and brother, and we will have peace."

Ibrahim coughed again, a weak cough. He told Yusuf the doctors would operate the next week, and he would have tubes down his throat and be unable to speak. "I use the solid gold pieces that go around the head to buy the bakery. Twelve pieces. There is enough left to buy the car washes and your plane ticket. There is more left, and I keep it, you know, for emergencies. Over $400 each ounce of gold in those days. Sixteen hundred dollar each ounce now in 2010! Can you imagine, boy? Four times more I must pay back! But this is God. In the Good Book it say thief must pay back five times. So I get off cheap, right?"

He stopped to take a breath and tried to smile.

"Each piece is many ounces. Long, spread out from head. From head." He reached behind his bald head and spread his fingers. "And open out like sun, Other pieces in cave not like these. They made of stone and gold foil cover on glass, not solid gold, so I only take twelve solid pieces. Ones around the holy head."

"It was your land," said Yusuf. "You had the right."

"No!" He coughed and coughed and spit into his sheet.

"But maybe God gave you the gold to help us get away from the war," Yusuf offered.

"Not mine! Belong to God. I should make sacrifice and find other way to come to USA. All these years, it is a knife in my heart. Take away the knife, Yusuf. Before I pass. I must trust you. Do this. You will do this, and God will see what you do for the old man. He will look at you. He will look at you."

+ + +

Was it a shout he heard? He listened through the downpour to the rush of the little torrent beside the cave. Thunder shouted across the valley.

He took another drink of wine and placed the bottle beside his feet. He loved this cave. He had brought back the twelve gold pieces, each an inch wide at its base, expanding to three inches and thickening at its top. After finding the cave, Yusuf had mortared all twelve into the old slots behind the head and cleaned and polished them. He had then called Uncle Ibrahim in Detroit. The old man must have been hanging on till he got that call, because he died within the week. But now all had been set right. Ibrahim's final peace was now Yusuf's to keep.

The rain was falling, and he felt sleep coming on.

+ + +

Years at the car washes. A teenager with wild red hair in a 57 Chevy wheels in during a driving rainstorm. Yusuf opens the sliding office window and asks, "You going to wash the car in this rain?"

"Man, your damned change machine ain't workin' again! Come on, here's five. You sand people can't keep your shit running." The boy reaches out his open window through the pelting rain with a five-dollar bill.

Yusuf takes the money.

"My dad wants the car spicked up before tonight."

Yusuf can see the boy's excitement.

"He's going to let me drive it, man. The rain'll stop, and I need to wax it tonight in our garage. Sun's supposed to come out tomorrow for the show. We're taking this to the car show, man. Come on! I've got to get on this!"

Yusuf slowly breaks open a paper cylinder of quarters and counts out twenty silver coins.

"Come on, man! I'm getting soaked out here!"

Somewhere a car honks, and Yusuf deliberately shovels the quarters onto the boy's wrist, letting them fall to the pavement where they bounce and scatter.

"What the hell?" the boy yells. "Get me my change!"

Yusuf slides the window shut and turns his back while the boy, cursing and yelling, gets out of his Chevy and picks up the coins in the rain, then slams his door shut and squeals his tires out of the lot and away.

The long days at the car washes had worn Yusuf down. A mindless job: fixing machines, replacing hoses, ordering soaps and waxes, dealing with irate customers. His anger wasn't what it used to be, but what anger remained was bad for business.

✦ ✦ ✦

Outside, lightning flashed, and thunder sounded. His eyes jerked open. He folded the last piece of his pita bread back into its cloth and slipped it into his jacket pocket. He took off his stocking cap and laid it beside him.

He heard a shout. Something falling, splashing. Thunder erupted just outside the cave. Someone yelled.

Yusuf jumped up. A dark figure leaned into the doorway, two hands reaching blindly into the darkness of the cave. Then the man's boot stepped forward but missed the step. His feet went out from under him and he landed on his butt. "Damn it to hell!" came a voice cursing in English. The man unshouldered his backpack. "Son of a bitch! This is going to kill me!" the man said.

Yusuf reached in his pocket for his matches and struck one to give the man light.

The stranger shouted and leaped back through the doorway, tripped over his backpack, and sprawled toward the drop-off but stopped himself by grabbing and tearing the old vines.

Yusuf laughed, holding the match at arm's length.

The man sat up, breathing hard, staring back into the darkness, staring at the flickering match. Rain and wind whipped along the cliffside, and water gushed down the channel nearby. The man put his hands down and pushed himself back through the doorway. "I can't get back to the trail," he gasped.

Yusuf said the storm would be over soon, and he could get back on the trail after the rain stopped. The man asked him how he knew English, and Yusuf said, "Car washes."

"Car washes?"

"I used to manage car washes in Detroit."

The match went out. Yusuf opened the box of matches and struck another. The man's round face and baseball cap appeared in the uncertain light. He was fiddling with the pockets of his backpack. Then he noticed the opposite bench, got up, and sat down on it, dragging the backpack to him and adjusted his baseball cap. "I'm a photographer for *Nat Geo*. That's what I'm up here for."

In the small light of the match, Yusuf could see something of his round head and bulky shoulders.

"The mountains are very beautiful," Yusuf said. The match burned near his fingers, and he shook it out and flicked it out the door. In the darkness, he heard the man fumbling with his backpack. Yusuf lit a third match. He watched the flame flare up and burn, casting its slight light on the two men.

"Not much money in car washes is there?" said the man.

"Not much. But my uncle paid me more than I was worth." He watched the match burn toward his fingers and turned it vertically. The flame slowly diminished and wisped out. He heard the man unzip his backpack, and then a light flashed on.

Yusuf stood up abruptly and stepped forward, holding up a hand. "No!" he said. "Not here!"

But the light swept across the back of the cave.

Yusuf could not see the face behind the glare of the flashlight, but he knew what was happening. He stepped forward and slapped at the flashlight, but the man was on his feet and passed the flashlight to his left hand, stiff-arming Yusuf with his right hand to keep him away.

Yusuf grabbed the arm and pushed hard. The man rolled into the stone bench on the opposite side of the entrance, and the beam of light jumped to the back of the cave.

Yusuf slapped hard at the flashlight.

The man cried out, "What the hell are you doing?"

"This," said Yusuf, "is private property. You have no right to be here. Get out of here!" Yusuf grabbed the man's soaked coat and tried to jerk him toward the doorway.

"Just let me see it!" The man's voice was a high, nervous tenor. "Please! Come on, man, let me see it!"

"You give me that flashlight and get the hell out of here!"

"Don't you know what you've got here!" the man cried. "A treasure! An absolute treasure. Let me just take a few pictures. I'm a photographer for Christ's sake!"

Yusuf put his shoulder into the man and shoved hard, but the man rolled sideways and they both stumbled, then pitched forward, stumbling together toward the back wall and slammed into stone. The flashlight clattered to the floor and rolled away, slinging its beam up and down the walls as it rolled over uneven stone.

"The photographer grabbed his forehead. "Damn!" he shouted. "You cracked my skull!" He pushed Yusuf away. "What's the matter with you! My head's bleeding."

"You! American! Get out of here."

Yusuf stepped in again and heaved the man back toward the doorway, lunging against his wet hulk, pushing with all he had.

The gasping, panting man was slippery with mud and heavy. The two of them staggered back to the doorway and struggled. Fear must have strengthened the man. With a roar, he gave Yusuf a mighty shove and cried out, "Come on, man! Let's talk about this. I don't want to take anything." He stepped forward, reached down, and grabbed the flashlight.

The beam darted to the back wall.

Yusuf, breathing heavily, backed away, turning to see the circle of light skitter over the stone walls of the cave and onto the shining glory of gold and glittering glass—over blue ripples layered into ivories, across flowing hues of purple, lavender, and lilac, rich reds draped in subtle folds falling from a shoulder and folding formally over the knees, the long fingers of one hand holding a great book marked in Greek letters, the lifted right hand with two raised fingers and a thumb. Above the regal shoulders and the brief formal beard, the face was complete. The mouth was there, the firm lips pressed together in solemn perfection, indigo eyes the color of dark grapes—intent, stern, taking in the gazers.

Yusuf looked at what he had long loved. One cheek and the side of the nose were in places missing the little stone pieces that formed the grand mosaic, but even these imperfections, these shadowed pits in the stone wall, seemed to mingle with the colored stones to add an earthy texture to the magisterial face.

"What a sight," breathed the photographer. "It must be sixth century. Better than the mosaics in Ravenna. Better than all of them. Such subtleties! Such workmanship. Look at the ivory. Look at the gold!" Twelve rays of solid, polished gold spread from behind the figure's head, their curved circumference forming the halo.

Suddenly the light of the flashlight dropped from the figure and scurried across the swept floor, then jumped again upon the regal face.

Yusuf stood there watching, his mind racing. It had been found. What could he do? The man would report this. He would let the world know.

"Look!" the man said as he approached the mosaic, speaking as if pointing out wonders to a friend. "Each stone fits the next." He moved closer. "And the stone smalti, beautiful shades of gray and white—dark blue around the golden halo and fading away to sky blue. Magnificent! I've never seen anything like it. It's as if the artist painted with stones. Such perfection!"

He was going on like this as Yusuf stood there, stiff, anxious, angry.

The photographer found the stone bench along the sidewall right beside Yusuf and sat down abruptly, toppling the wine bottle on the floor. It rolled away over the uneven stone, pouring out its contents. "Oh, sorry," the photographer said. Reaching down, he retrieved the half-filled bottle. He set it back down on the floor, but his eyes were on the mosaic. "Did I knock those pieces out when I fell against it?" The beam of light had landed again on the face.

"They did not fall out because of your soft head, American."

The circle of light darted across the six-foot figure on the wall and then dropped again to the floor. "There! A little stack of pieces. Did you do that?" The light skipped onto Yusuf's weathered face.

"Shut it off."

After a moment, the light clicked into darkness.

Outside, wind and heavy rain. Inside, they could still hear the mad torrent washing down near the cave and leaping over the brink while slowly a grey light seemed to spread through the cave as their eyes adjusted. There was the smell of the spilled wine.

The tenor voice sounded from the darkness. "You're trying to piece together the losses in the face?"

"I have been trying to piece myself together," said Yusuf.

The photographer said nothing for a moment. "Had any luck putting the pieces back?"

"It is not a matter of luck."

"Not a matter of luck!"

Yusuf said nothing.

"Don't you believe in luck? Look at me. I'm Mr. Luck himself!" He stood up from the bench and shuffled toward the back of the cave. "Doctor Luck! King of all possible luck! I thought I was a dead man, slipping off that trail and getting washed over the cliff with the lightning blasting all around me. I swear, I thought I was a stone-blind goner. Absolutely done for. And look! I've found more than I could ever hope to . . ." He stopped, and Yusuf could hear him panting near the icon. He must have been running his hands over the mosaic. "This is going to make me famous—*us* famous," came the voice. "*National Geographic, Archaeology Today*, Italian magazines, British, French. . . . And

Polish. You know there's a new market for this shit in Poland? This will make the covers of all the magazines."

"No."

"What do you mean, no? This will pay. You want a cut, no problem. No problem at all. I'll have the magazine sign a contract."

Yusuf heard the man's shuffling steps move back to the opposite bench. "It *is* a problem," said Yusuf. "I look at him, and he looks at me, and I am lost in the looking."

"Thousands! That's what I'm talkin' about. Thousands and more thousands. Do you have any idea what magazines will pay for a discovery like this? Archaeologists are going to be thunderstruck, man! My girlfriend won't believe it. She said I was crazy going into Lebanon. They kidnap Americans in Lebanon, she said. But I told her, I told her, no, no. Not anymore. And I'll stick to the little Christian valleys—stay away from the Hezbollah, the Druse, the Sunnis, and Shi'ites. You see, I do my research before I do a photo shoot."

"This place is not for sale."

"Of course, of course. I'm not asking to buy the cave, just the photos."

"Thieves will come for the gold," said Yusuf. "The thieves will come over the mountains, and in one night, they will destroy the holy face."

"Holy? holy? Yeah, it's got a few pieces missing, but it's the best damned mosaic I have ever laid eyes on. It's buried treasure is what it is."

Then the flashlight clicked on again, and the light scuttled over the mosaic. Once again the colors spoke into the darkness.

"Bee-yoo-tee-ful . . . my God!" said the man. The light clicked off.

His voice came again. "Look, I can see you value this place. Don't want people stealing your shit. I understand that. But believe me, you can make some serious cash out of a find like this. Make it a tourist destination or something. There's people down in Jezzine will help you out. Like the mayor. I talked to him this morning, had breakfast. Seems like a real reasonable man."

"The mayor, others, will make demands."

The photographer continued. "Look, believe me, this is your lucky day. I'm serious, I don't want to take this from you. I just want a few pics, and then I'll be on my way. Look, I don't even have to tell people where this place is at. The mystery might actually bring more attention."

"The magazine people will make you tell them. They will find this place. Write stories about it. It is very old."

"Yeah, old. Old. Absolutely amazing! Look at it! How can you keep it all to yourself?" The flashlight clicked on again.

Yusuf took a deep breath and looked at the icon.

Then the photographer knelt beside his backpack and pulled something out. He turned suddenly toward the back of the cave and flashed a picture.

Yusuf stood up. "No. I said no!" He reached for the camera, but the photographer jerked away and flashed another picture.

Yusuf's fists closed tight. He swung hard, and his right fist broke on the man's forehead. Yusuf shouted in pain as the photographer's knees buckled, and the man sat down hard on the cave floor as Yusuf staggered back to his bench and sat down, holding his right wrist tight.

He saw the man slowly sit up in the doorway, a silhouette against the grey light of the storm. The flashlight was somehow still trained on the mosaic.

The man seemed to be speaking in a dream, his high voice still analyzing the icon: "Did you see that? Halo gold . . . glass red . . . red white. . . nimbus or stone some . . ." The man's breath came in short gasps. His hand strayed absently up to his forehead as if he hadn't even noticed the blow.

Yusuf was in agony. Holding his broken hand, his anger burning.

"It's as if the artist painted with stones," the man whispered. " I've got to get it for every . . ." The man turned the flashlight off once again, and almost immediately the camera flashed again.

Yusuf stood, stepped forward as another flash went off. The face at the back of the cave leaped out of the darkness: the indigo eyes, the stern mouth—and vanished. Yusuf stopped, stepped back to the stone bench, and sat down. He stared at the man in the pale grey light from the cave's mouth as he knelt and began shooting pictures from every angle pos-sible—standing up, going down on one knee and shooting, prostrating himself on the floor and shooting, grunting as he pushed himself to his feet and shooting, shuffling left and shooting, right and shooting, rising again and shooting, shooting as if engaged in some strange and elaborate ritual. The bright flashes of the camera blinded them both, the colors exploding then going black, exploding and vanishing. Thirty, forty spasms of light shot through the small sanctuary, and each time the gold-haloed Christ, his royal robes, his great book, his raised hand, sprang from the darkness and returned to silence.

Yusuf watched, his heart pounding, his anger rising. Outside the wind and the rain raged, and the mad little torrent leapt over the brink of the cliff into empty space.

The man was relentless. Flash after thunderless flash flooded the room.

When his acquisitions were at last complete, he turned to Yusuf and said in that high, excited voice, "That's enough for now. I'm sure I've got it."

Yusuf watched.

"Look, we can keep this kind of hush-hush. I won't be any trouble. Believe me, this will make my career. And it can make yours too. I'll just slip away when the rain stops, and you can keep this for yourself."

"Sit down. We talk," Yusuf said.

The figure reached back for the wall and stepped back to the stone bench on the opposite wall. He sat.

Yusuf began: "I have lost my wife. This is all I have now. The orchards and this quiet place. It is a place of rest. I am the protector. For this, I was sent. If you take those pictures—"

"Look, I think I understand. You're not into this for the money. I can go with that. I'm not really into photography for the money either. I mean, I just love the pictures, the travel—it's a kind of art, you know—photography. Like this mosaic is art.

"It is more than art, American."

"Philip," the man said. "It's Philip." He stood and reached out to shake Yusuf's hand in the darkness, but Yusuf ignored it.

The man sat back down.

"Yeah, I get it," said the man. "More than art. It's, like, some private space for you or something."

The rain was falling steadily now. Muffled thunder was moving away up the valley. The soft light had returned. Yusuf looked at the dark figure with the boyish face hunched over on the bench.

"But shouldn't this be available to everybody?' the man said.

"I mean, it's like a church. Just the last couple of weeks, I was snapping pics of little French churches for *National Geographic*. Those priests and nuns don't have any problems with pictures."

"I have told no one of this place."

"But, man, art like this should be open to the world. Look at King Tut and all that. Art for the world, man."

Yusuf said nothing.

"Think of those cave paintings in France, man, or the cathedrals. Why should you be the only one to see this?"

The water outside in the channel had subsided to a lapping and gurgling. A quiet rain fell slanting across the mouth of the cave.

"I have thought of this," said Yusuf. "But here, the silent one looks at me, and I am found in his looking."

The photographer said nothing for a while.

"But someone's going to find this sooner or later."

"Someone has just found it."

"Yeah, yeah. I guess so. But man, I won't do any damage. I'll get this in the best, the very best magazines."

Yusuf could hear distant thunder. The tapping of rain on leaves near the mouth of the cave. They both sat in silence.

"Well," said the photographer after a few moments, "I promise you, I will not tell a soul where this place is at. I swear to it. Nobody. It's okay, man, if that's what you want."

Yusuf sat in stony silence, his quick breaths coming and going.

"One more thing," the man said. "Just one. I mean this just hit me. To get the full effect, you'd have to light this thing up. I mean all that beauty can't be stuck there in the dark."

The flashlight clicked on again. It darted over the icon to the surrounding stone. It quickly alighted on small stone shelves on either side of the mosaic that held little clay lamps, no more than blackened clay dishes pinched on one side to hold a wick in the oil.

"There! There, and yes, there! Four of em! The light beam slid quickly across the walls. "And more! How many? We'll need to fire those up to get the full effect, to get the original effect, you know. I've got a tripod here, so I can shoot in low light. We've got to do this."

"We?" Yusuf's anger was rising. "I don't work for you, American."

"Absolutely! Absolutely, man. But I'll be out of here soon. Vamoosed. Gone like a shout in the dark."

The flashlight was trained on the icon again. Yusuf looked at it and waited. There was still the smell of spilled wine. The soft patter of rain. The bright glow of the halo. The dark eyes of the icon were intense.

His broken knuckles were throbbing, but he stood slowly and stepped to the nearest olive-oil lamp. The man was too heavy to throw out. He would have to wait till the man was leaving. Yusuf took his box of matches from his jacket pocket with his left hand, held the box awkwardly in his broken right hand, extracted a match, struck it, then held it to the lamp wick.

Slowly he moved from one lamp to the next. The smell of sulphur from the matches mingled with the smell of the spilled red wine, and now there was the added scent of incense, for he had bought powdered incense from Yemen and had mixed it with the oil. He lit the seventh lamp and returned to his bench. Meanwhile the photographer had been hurriedly setting up his tripod, placing his camera and screwing it down tight, setting the aperture and clicking through the settings.

The photographer was right. The mellow lamplight transmuted the mosaic; the fierce indigo eyes seemed to soften, the face calmed, the red scar in the palm of the raised hand deepened. The whole figure shone with a gentle radiance, the individualized pieces of stone and glass and gold blending into the human figure, the flames lending a flickering life.

Ten minutes later, the photographer was finished. He knelt to unscrew the camera and fold the tripod, inserting them into the pockets of the backpack.

The light outside had brightened with the passing of the storm front. Yusuf could see the man's face clearly for the first time as he worked to put everything away. A round, sunburned, boyish face with his baseball cap turned sideways on his head so he could look through the camera's eyepiece. In the lamplight, Yusuf could see fine wrinkles around his eyes, a pale double chin. A darker welt was swelling above an eyebrow where Yusuf had hit him.

He remembered taking Amy to a Detroit Tigers baseball game, her baseball cap turned sideways on her head because, she told him, she had seen it in a magazine, and it was cute sideways. He remembered her high ten-year-old voice, her excitement as the players ran onto the field. He remembered looking at her that day, wanting to give her the world, but never finding the words to tell her.

"I'll get this in the best, the very best magazines. But I swear, I won't tell anybody where it's at. Zilcho. Nada. I'll keep my lips zipped."

Yusuf listened to the outrageous contradiction of those words. He took a deep breath, stood up, and positioned himself to shove the man out as he left. His heart was pounding. He felt the heavy, heavy weight of what he was about to do. It was a two-hundred-foot drop outside the cave. It should shatter the camera, but what if it did not? He would have to climb down the cliff and find it, destroy it, then report the man's death.

The man shouldered his backpack and turned to go but paused and turned for a last look at the icon. His gaze turned Yusuf's nervous eyes, and they both stood there gazing again at the lamplit glass and the gold, the colored pieces of blue shading into cerulean, magenta rising into scarlet, ivories folding into creams, and tans into ochers that followed the folds of the linen garments, the scarred hand with its glow of red raised in blessing. Their eyes were drawn again to the gold rays surrounding the royal dignity of the face, the indigo eyes almost brown in the lamplight.

The photographer seemed unable to leave, but at last he nodded at Yusuf, then turned to go. He stepped up the first step to the mouth of the cave.

Yusuf stepped forward.

The man stopped and looked back at the great puzzle.

Yusuf stopped. His breath came in rapid, shallow gasps. He could see the young man's face clearly now, turned toward the image: the round cheeks, the sideways cap, eyes wide in the lamplight, the parted mouth, the rise and fall of the man's breathing.

The photographer stood on the first step for some time, staring at the mosaic as if trying to decipher something, his hand straying to the growing lump on his forehead. He stood long enough to turn Yusuf's gaze back to the image. There was a lamplit flicker of red in the wounded hand. Then Yusuf's eyes caught the same flicker of light in the steady gaze of the dark brown eyes and suddenly understood that those silent eyes had long been speaking to him. Had long evoked the intense but silent suffering of his mother's eyes on that fateful day in his youth.

The photographer glanced back at Yusuf and nodded. "Thanks, man," he said. "I appreciate it. I really do."

Yusuf could see the young man's face turned toward him, a dark silhouette with just a glimmer of candlelight in his eyes.

The man turned in the doorway and ducked out.

Yusuf heard his boots shuffling along the ledge, then splashing up the channel.

He stood for several seconds, his heart pounding, staring out the mouth of the cave at the light rain falling across the mountain valley, the wash of faded blues and greens across the opposite slopes.

Yusuf, protector of the sanctuary, caretaker of orchards and of sacred visions, sat down heavily on his bench, leaned back against the stone wall, took a deep breath, and closed his eyes. After a moment, Yusuf the grudging giver released his breath and sat listening to the quiet fall of the good rain. His left hand pushed delicately at the broken knuckles of his right hand.

After a while, Yusuf leaned down and picked up the almost-empty bottle of wine and poured the last of the wine slowly onto the floor. He held the bottle till the last drop fell.

PUZZLE

They feel a bump, and the train begins rolling out of New York City's Penn Station a few minutes after four on a July afternoon. They have found seats near the back of the third car.

Philip turns to Isabelle and says, "Well, Izzy, are you excited about heading off into the vast unknown?"

"Excited? Not the word I'd use."

"What then?"

"Scared."

"Quiet Kansas doesn't scare you," he says. "You've been living in New York City, for God's sake. Five whole years in the big city."

"It's the quiet that scares me," she says. "I hate being bored. I had enough of it growing up in little Wellsville."

He places his laptop between his legs on the floor. "Bore-*doom*," he says, "the great enemy of humanity."

"Ohio, Indiana, Illinois, Kansas," she says. "I've never been west of the Adirondacks. I don't much care to travel the blandscape."

"Blandscape," he says. "How about tiny Wellsville, New York, where you grew up?"

"At least we had forests. And hills."

He looks past her to the passing city. "I loved Kansas when I was a boy. Maybe you can try for an open mind."

She smiles, leans against his shoulder, and lays a hand on his hand. "I *am* glad to take this trip with you. Without our rush-around schedules. I've been looking forward to it. Glad we didn't take a plane, babe."

"Me too. I like the train." He places his other hand on hers, intersecting her fingers. They listen to the gathering acceleration of the train, the hum and rumble and clicks. A few seats ahead, a baby squeals; across the aisle a couple talks in a language he can't place.

"So," he says, "I've been waiting for this time together to ask you something."

She looks at him.

"Something's been driving me crazy. Like a cricket in the corner."

"A cricket in the corner?"

"Never had a corner cricket? You start working on something or you're reading a book or watching television on some quiet night and some damn cricket starts its loud chirping, and there's no way to find the little bastard. It's behind the baseboard or in a cabinet. You stomp around, and it quits till you sit back down. Then it starts up again."

"No, babe. Can't say I remember something like that. Maybe it's a Kansas thing."

He glances around the Amtrak car. Quite a crowd. Half the people on their phones, a few staring out the windows, the man and his wife across the aisle speaking maybe an African dialect? He turns and kisses the top of her head and catches the scent of her shampoo.

She begins taking the band out of her ponytail.

He watches her. Black hair. Black as a murder of crows, he thinks. He loves that phrase. You're supposed to say raven hair, but what the hell makes a raven anymore lovely than a collection of crows? He remembers a winter afternoon wandering the Kansas Flint Hills with his .22 rifle, watching black crows catch a sleet-blowing north wind: rising high, cawing, hurtling straight down into leafless oaks along a hillside, then up again, shouting their joy, loving the wild weather, loving every minute of their short, ridiculous lives. So, crow black it is. Hair as black as a murder of crows. And a sharp face, dark eyes. Eyes like obsidian when she's mad, but beautiful, beautiful in every way, he thinks. He was surprised that day in the storefront gallery when she turned those eyes from his photographs on display and noticed him, a tall, dumpy, round-shouldered guy, dressed spiffy that day in a white shirt and a deep blue, star-sprinkled tie for the display of his photographs of Dakota gas fields, treeless prairies, distant thunderstorms. At the time, he assumed she liked, maybe respected his photos. But she had persisted. He has come to like that word *persist*.

"I haven't told a soul about this," he says.

"A recent secret?"

"Since I returned from France and Lebanon."

She starts brushing out her shoulder-length hair. "Three months and you haven't told me?"

"Something I found in Lebanon."

She stops brushing. "A girl?"

"No, no. Nothing like that. Why would you say that?"

She smiles. "Then why keep your crazy little cricket to yourself for three months?"

"I found something."

She starts brushing again.

"A cave." He pauses as a large woman pulling a toddler by the hand passes them in the aisle, heading back toward the restrooms. "I took pictures."

"You're a photographer, Philip. *National Geographic* was paying you to take pictures."

"There was a problem."

She stops brushing her hair.

"Here's the story. A storm blew up the valley from behind me as I was hiking up this mountain trail in south Lebanon to snap a few landscape photos. A tough trail it was, Izzy. Up and down, pine forest on my left, a straight drop-off of maybe 300 feet down to a mountain stream on my right. I'm not in good enough shape to take on a trail like that, but after getting pics of the city of Jezzine and of a few churches and a monastery, I needed some really photogenic landscapes. So I was panting my way up that twisty little dirt trail."

She nods and places the brush in her lap.

"Then rain and wind caught up with me along that ridge. Lightning started cracking around me. Not as bad as a lot of Kansas thunderbusters, but, hell, bad enough. I was soaked in seconds. Heavy rain, but my camera was in the backpack, so I was okay.

"But that cliff beside me had me spooked. I was watching my steps. Suddenly the trail drops into a little washout, and I slip on wet clay or something and splash down hard into storm water just pouring down and running right out over that cliff. I yell like crazy and start grabbing for anything, the water washing me down a few yards to that hellacious drop-off that'll kill me. A bolt of lightning explodes beside me, and I went deaf with my hands grabbing everywhere, and it was like the whole world had gone silent and was in slow motion as I smashed through bushes at the cliff edge." He looks at her dark eyes watching him.

"I managed somehow to latch onto a handful of leaves and branches as the water went pouring out over that cliff, and I swung over the edge and pulled myself flat up against the rock by these breaking branches, and my feet somehow found a ledge, and I sidestepped quick along it and ducked under a big shelf of stone and into an opening that turned out to be a cave."

He looks at her again.

"Why haven't you told me this story?"

"I *am* telling you."

"You've asked me to marry you, Philip. I might want to know of your near-death experiences without waiting months."

"I know, I know. So I've been holding off till we could talk alone."

"We've had all kinds of time to talk alone. We've been sleeping together, Philip."

"Yeah, well. There's this problem, and I wanted to run it by you at a time when we can focus."

"Focus."

"Yes, Izzy. Concentrate. So, to continue. I jerk myself into the cave and sit down hard. Everything in there dark. I can't hear anything, not even the storm. I can't see anything. I'm blind as a rock and deaf."

Her hand finds his leg again. She's wearing a white t-shirt and khaki shorts.

He places his hand on her knee and takes another breath. "So I'm sitting there in the mouth of this cave feeling like the mountain has swallowed me whole, and I'm trying to get my shit together when a light flares up two or three feet from my face. That was a shock, Izzy, shock after shock. I mean, I thought I was a dead man going over that cliff, then the next second I'm in this cave sitting down hard on my tailbone, and then this flare-up of a light in front of my nose just as I'm dropping my backpack from my shoulders. I yelped and jumped backwards, almost went out the cave mouth and over the cliff.

"About this time there's another blast of lightning outside and some guy laughs. So obviously my hearing has come back. I notice that there's a hand holding a burning match maybe three feet from my nose, and it's then, Izzy, it's then that I catch first sight of a quick glimmer of something twenty feet back in the cave. There must have been another flash of lightning because I can't see how that one match would light up the back of the cave. Something back there. And then I see a face move near the match, and it's this guy calling me an American. I can hear his voice, but I can't see his face."

"How did he know you were American?"

"I don't know. Maybe I was swearing or screaming some shit. So he strikes another match, and I can see something of this Lebanese guy's face: biggish nose, long jaw. Dark hair. Seems to be smiling."

"Then the match goes out. It's black as hell in there again, but my eyes are gradually adjusting to the light. I get up and sit on this bench opposite the man."

"There were benches?"

"Two stone benches nicely carved out of rock, one on either side of the entry . . . then the drop-off."

She nods.

"At some point, the match goes out and he lights up another, and my eyes are adjusting. He's a middle-aged guy. I ask him how he knows English. He says he lived in Detroit. Managed some car washes in the area. He doesn't say anything for a while, and I can't see in the shadowy light if he's nodding or smiling or what. I tell him I'm a photographer on a gig for *National Geographic.*

"He says the mountains are beautiful, and his match burns out. Anyway, it's pitch black in there again so I'm feeling for my backpack to find my flashlight, but he strikes another match and holds it between us. I say something about there not being much money in car washes, and he says his uncle or friend or somebody paid him pretty well, and I watch him turn the match and watch the light burn down. His eyes are on the fire. Then it goes out, and I find the flashlight and click it on, and this Lebanese guy who's been so nice and quiet all of a sudden jumps up and goes ape-shit mad. Starts slapping hard at the flashlight and yelling no, no, and I'm sliding away along the bench, and the light from my flashlight finds the back wall of that cave. I can't see what it is in that flash, but there are these colors. And he's getting all violent, and I stand up and shove him back, and my light runs across the rough cave walls back to the colors, but he obviously doesn't want me to see what's there."

"What was it? Guns? Grenades?"

"No, no, nothing like that. But then he's on me, and it turns out I'm a real horse in a fight, Izzy, and he's lean and mean but no match. So we're cabbaged onto each other and go stumbling back into the cave, and my head slams hard into the back of the cave, and I yell some choice words, and we kind of wrestle around, and I'm roaring like a bull, and we stumble back to the entry, and the thought of that cliff comes to mind, so I get a hand on his face and shove hard, and I sit back down hard on those steps again. My tailbone was bruised for a month."

"Steps in the cave?"

"Yeah. Carved steps, like the benches. I'm thinking he's going to come at me again to push my carcass right on out of the cave, so my adrenaline is pumping, and then I see the flashlight lying on the floor, so I must have dropped it. Anyway, I crawl over and snatch it up, and I'm expecting this guy to jump me again, but he doesn't. Sometime during the rumble, I must have knocked his wine bottle over. I can't remember if I picked it up or he did, but you could smell the wine. Spilled it all over the stone floor. Anyway, when I shine the beam on the back wall, he just stops moving. Stays put and stares at what I'm staring at."

"He was trying to kill you! What was he hiding?"

The train is swaying slightly, the regular low rumble and clicks of the train on tracks moving rhythmically as they pass over the wide Hudson River. Her hand slides into his. "What was he hiding, Phil?"

"I don't know."

"You don't know?"

"I don't know if I can tell you."

"What was it? Stolen stuff?" She gives his hand a squeeze.

"What? No."

"What, then? Drugs?"

"No, nothing like that."

"Well, why would you keep it from me? We talk about everything."

"It's a secret."

"That's no good, Phillip." She removes her hand and sits back in her seat. "You've asked me to marry you. You're taking me to meet your parents. Why did you keep something like this from me?"

"I think I know what you'll say."

"My God, Philip. Don't act like I'm a child." She picks up the hairbrush. "I'm your friend and lover. If you can't trust me, what are we doing?"

He sits in silence. After a while, the woman and her toddler pass them in the aisle and return to their seats.

"Izzy, I feel like a ground squirrel in a wire cage."

"A what?" She grabs the last six inches of her hair and begins brushing it out in short, fierce strokes.

"I'll explain. I'll explain. My dad trapped one of those little striped ground squirrels on the farm once when I was five or six. He tacked some chicken wire over a wooden box. Thought it would make a nice pet for me, but every time I came into its line of sight, it would leap straight up into the wire till its little nose was all bloody. Every time my head appeared over the box, the little sucker went off like a spring-loaded mechanism. Whap! Right into the chicken wire. Again and again. We had to let him go. . . . So where was I?"

"The mystery cave."

"Okay, yes. I was afraid the Lebanese guy would catch his wind and jump me again, so I reached into my backpack while the man was staring at the back wall and grabbed old Betsy, snapped off her lens cover and flashed a picture. Then, bam! He takes a swing at me. Next thing I know, I'm on my butt for the third time. I see the guy off to the side, mooing like a castrated calf; I think he broke his hand on my hard head. Anyway, I got a bump on my head that gave me a strange look all the way back to New York. You remember?"

"You said you bumped it on a wall."

"Which I did."

"What was it, Philip? What was he hiding? He was a terrorist or something?"

"No, no. Nothing like that."

"Then tell me! Why are you keeping this from me?"

"Whap! Into the chicken wire I go again. Come on, give me some space here. I'll try to get this out." He pauses and stares out the window, seeing nothing but the cave. He continues: "So this guy obviously loves this cave. Mentioned something about finally finding some peace there. He didn't use those words, but my mind was galloping uphill, and I can't remember what he said exactly, but the impressions were clicking into place in my head; you know what I mean? Something about peace and after landing in that cave, I could see something of what he meant. I mean, storm howling outside. Quiet inside."

"He loves a cave. Okay. So why does that mean he can kill you?"

"He loves what's in it."

She waits. Her hands start turning, twisting her hairbrush in her lap.

Philip gets up suddenly and heads down the aisle toward the restroom. He finds it, slides the door open and steps in. A sink, a mirror, a toilet. The practical necessities. He sits down on the toilet lid. The rumble of the train is louder in there. One sentence he tries to remember. The man had said, "The silent one looks at me . . . "

He stands up and stares into the mirror, looking right through himself. For the thousandth time, he begins reconsidering her concerns. Her father Jose is a school janitor thirty years out of El Salvador. Found a job cleaning a middle school in Wellsville. A quiet man with a heavy accent who, on first meeting Philip, had asked right away about Philip's father, who is a rancher in southern Kansas: Why wasn't Philip working for his father? Philip told him his older brother Bob was inheriting the ranch, and Philip couldn't see working for his bossy brother. So Jose asked him if he could possibly make a living as a photographer. He had told this janitor that he thought a man should follow what he loves, follow his dreams, the old American schtick. Jose had raised his graying eyebrows at that comment. He is a hardworking man. Isabelle had filled him in about her father's work: he is good at cleaning up carpets after vomit, hard wads of gum stuck under seats or ground into tile floors, at dealing with locked doors, broken bicycle chains, broken noses, and sobbing seventh graders. Her mother Mirabella cleans homes part-time now that the kids are out of the house. Isabella is their third child, the first to go to college, where she began by studying art on a partial scholarship, but her father and mother talked her into a more practical degree: elementary education. She loves art. Now she's been teaching for two years in a charter school in New York City that allows her to use her art interests in the classroom, but she doesn't like dealing with excitable, rebellious sixth graders. Still, a job is a job, she says, "My parents need to think about retirement, not supporting their little *muchachita*."

The one thing her mother Mirabella had asked him on that visit was, "You like the bébés?"

"Which babies?" he had stupidly asked.

She had laughed. "You bébés. My grandbébés."

He had laughed too. "Oh sure, sure. I like babies. I think I can talk Isabelle into having a baby eventually. We'll take care of that problem when it comes."

Of course, her mom had fired back with "*Problemo? Que problemo?*"

Philip's first assignment with *National Geographic* has been a terrific boost to his prospects, and to Isabelle's. But now this. He turns on the water and splashes cold water on his face and looks into the mirror without reaching for a paper towel. The water drips down his wide cheeks as he stares through the mirror.

Isabelle has lived poor all her life and has developed a practical mind, knows how to get by, thinks up strategies for advancement. She was the one who bumped into a *National Geographic* photographer at an art show. She was cute enough to get the guy interested in arranging a meeting for her with the photographer's own contacts, who examined his portfolio and got him his first tentative assignment with *National Geographic*. Before departing for France and Lebanon, while riding that high, he had asked her to marry him. No ring to offer her, few prospects but this one trip and the photos not yet taken.

He remembers that moment: candle-lit dinner, dark wine in their glasses, quiet Italian restaurant, Frank Sinatra on the music system. He had arranged with the restaurant manager to play a Glen Campbell song at precisely 9:00 p.m. So he was pouring her another glass of Chianti when poor old Frank gets cut off halfway through a song, and good old Glen starts up with that famous song of his—almost the only country-western song Isabelle actually likes: *It's knowing that your door is always open/ And your path is free to walk. . .* He's memorized the lyrics and sometimes even plucks it out on his guitar and sings it for her: *That keeps you in the backroads/ By the rivers of my memory/ That keeps you ever gentle on my mind.*

When that song came on, she had looked up at the speakers, then across the candle-lit table at him, lifting her eyebrows like her father does. Then she caught on and smiled, and he popped the question, after which she had looked long into his anxious eyes and finally said, "I think so. Let's see how things go for six months." A practical woman.

He wipes the water from his face with his hands, opens the door, and walks back down the aisle wiping wet hands on his jeans.

Her head is turned away. She's staring out the window and won't look at him.

He sits down. "Okay, here's the deal," he says. "If anyone finds out what's in that cave, they will track me down and sort out my itinerary if necessary and set out to find it. They will find the man and his cave."

She keeps watching the passing buildings, but says, "This man is like, some kind of criminal? Some kind of terrorist?"

"No, no, no. I told you he's not."

She turns on him. "Then tell me! I'm not going to sit here and keep guessing. What did you do with the pics? Are they on your laptop?"

"Yes."

"Then if you don't have the nerve to tell me, just show me

the photos and let me decide for myself."

"You'll like the photos," he says. But he doesn't move to reach beneath his legs for his laptop.

"Well?"

"You have to swear to secrecy."

"What difference does it make if I swear? Swear to who? I don't believe in sacred oaths. But I'll give you my promise." She takes a deep breath. "That good enough for you?"

"You won't want to keep that promise."

"If you want me to keep the promise, I'll keep the promise. That's that. What on earth is the matter with you?"

"You don't understand."

"Of course I don't understand! Good God, you're driving me crazy, Philip! Why won't I understand?"

"Because you love me."

She stares into his round face, his flushed cheeks, his troubled eyes. After a few seconds, she says, "I do love you." She leans into him again and picks up his hand in both of hers.

"You'll want to break the promise,' he says, "for my sake."

He waits for her response.

"Come on, Philly. Fess up." She smiles.

He forces a smile and looks out the window. He thinks they're approaching Newark by now. They should be in Ohio by nightfall, and he has reserved what Amtrak calls a roomette: two bunk beds in a tiny room. But he intends to talk this out before sleeping.

After a minute she says, "Show me if you want. Don't show me if you want. Whatever." She drops his hand and turns back to the window.

He reaches for the laptop case, unzips it, extracts the laptop, replaces the case between his legs on the floor, opens the laptop on his knees. and punches the power button.

A few clicks and the file opens to a landscape of Lebanese mountains: rocky peaks, forested slopes. He feels her eyes on the screen.

One more click and there will be two people who have seen the photo.

He taps the file. It opens.

She looks at it for a few seconds. Then looks up at him. "Very nice," she says.

"Do you see it?"

"Of course I see it. It's beautiful. Excellent work. Like all your best photographs. I like the angle of the shot from just below and to the left. The colors are exquisite. It's really a great shot. You're really good at this, Philip."

"It's not about the quality of the photograph, for God's sake. I don't give a shit about the quality of the photo."

"Why not? What did your editors think of it?"

"No one has seen this but me and now you."

"Why not? What's the deep dark secret, Philly? I was thinking this was some kind of, like, shock, and now this?" She smiles and starts brushing her hair again. "The only mystery here is your mind, Philly."

"Don't call me Philly. A filly is a horse."

"You said you're as strong as a horse." She smiles again and taps his shoulder with her hairbrush.

"It's a female horse."

"What's wrong with female horses?"

"My dad's a rancher. You don't call boys girls."

"So, a horse is a horse, of course of course."

"Come on! This is no time for jokes."

"Philip, I've seen icons before. So it's a pretty spectacular one, I'll admit, and a very good photograph, lighting just right, a kind of candle glow or something picking up the mellow colors. And the rock, rough whitish rock shoving up around the face and shoulders, like the man is coming right out of the rock. I think it's a spectacular pic. Why not try it out on your editor? She'll love it."

Philip lets out his breath. "It's the best icon I've ever seen, Izzy. Better than the sixth-century Ravenna mosaics. Better than anything in Rome or Istanbul. Exquisite work."

"Okay. So it's a beautiful icon. Of a king, right? Do you know which king?"

"Which king? He's holding a book. He's got a halo. Who do you think he is?"

"Okay. So he's a king saint or something. I thought the halo was a crown."

"He's *the* king, Izzy."

"Okay. So is this a part of a church or monastery or something?"

"That's just it, Izzy. It's in this hidden cave. Apparently, no one knows about it but that Lebanese dude. That's the deal, Izzy. No one knows about this, and it must date from over a thousand years ago. It's old. Ancient. I've been studying icons like crazy these last three months. Maybe it goes right back to the sixth century when the Ravenna mosaics were done, and notice that halo or halo-crown, whatever it is."

He spreads the screen so that it magnifies the mosaic face, tiny black granules that line an eye, narrow, dark-brown stones that form an eyebrow, pale tan stones that fit precisely together to form the lighter flesh of the forehead. He moves the image so that it centers on the halo that radiates in expanding gold rays from behind the brown and black pieces that represent the man's hair. Each ray is a single, wedge-shaped plank of polished gold that spreads from behind the head, joining in a perfect semicircle around the head. The gold circle disappears behind the white robe of the right shoulder, the scarlet shoulder sash on the left.

"Very nice," she says. "Really remarkable."

"Solid gold," he says.

"What? The halo?"

"The twelve rays are solid gold, while the belt across his chest is made of these little squares called smalti: gold foil sealed in glass that the ancient iconographers used to save on expenses, but the rays themselves look like solid gold, thick, maybe a quarter-inch thick each, maybe more, thicker at the circumference, pressed into mortar. That's why they project from the blue squares surrounding them. Do you see how they come from behind the head and kind of lean out so the halo has this three-dimensional effect?"

"Expensive," she says.

"Very, very expensive."

"So was the man in the cave a security guard or something?"

"He owns the cave. No one knows it's there but him. I think I believe him."

"No one?"

"Such an ancient beautiful icon in such an unusual style would attract scholars, artists, tourists from all over the world if it were known. The style is similar to sixth-century icons, but the halo is unique. Anyway, most icons from the area were destroyed during the iconoclastic controversy way back in the 700s when the emperors of Byzantium abolished church art for maybe a hundred years. There's nothing like this one that I've found in the whole world. Maybe it comes from before icon styles were fixed. I've been doing a hell of a lot of googling and snooping in the big libraries, talking to a couple of professors of ancient history."

She sits back in the seat. "So *Nat Geo* doesn't know about this? You haven't showed it to them?"

"Of course not. They would right away send a writer to report on it. They would send scholars to study it, date it. It would make the cover of the magazine. Then the tourists would come."

"What's wrong with that?"

"The owner doesn't want it to be a tourist trap. I told him this could bring in thousands of bucks, and he said, 'Not for sale, American,' or something like that. I told him I'd split the proceeds from my photos, sign a contract. He said, 'This is a holy place, or face, something like that.' Which kind of flustered me. I mean I don't even know what that means."

"But tourists visit churches all over Europe and check out the art. In the Middle East too. Who doesn't allow that? Don't be crazy, Philip."

"He said that if it were known, thieves or political radicals would come for the gold. He's probably right about that in such a politically unstable country as Lebanon. Hezbollah, ISIS, Shiites, Sunnis, Druse, even common criminals. Who would protect it?"

"Maybe the churches of the area?"

"Maybe, but the owner is against letting them have it. He

doesn't trust the local mayor. Probably afraid he'll lose control of the place."

"But the owner could make money on it too," she says.

"That's not his wish."

"His wish? *Wish* is, like, a weak word, Phil. Doesn't the world have a right to see such a historic discovery? This is really exciting, babe. This could make your career."

"That's what I said to him! I knew then in my gut that this would make my career. A mosaic over a thousand years old discovered accidentally by little old me." He sits back and stares up the aisle. "*National Geo* wasn't thrilled with the pics I got in France. The weather wasn't right: clouds, rain. So I hurried off to southern Lebanon on their expense account to get pictures of the old Melkite and Maronite churches and monasteries, and those pics are fine. Got a good few of the great waterfall of Jezzine, and of some of the old churches built like forts, *Saydet Jezzine, Saydet Maabour, saydet* this and *saydet* that, shots from a limestone tower on top of which is this huge statue of the Virgin Mary looking calmly out over the mountain valley. The light was right in Lebanon. So the magazine said they might be interested in doing a little piece on that area. 'Might be interested' probably means they are not interested."

"Philip. This picture *would* launch your career."

"I know, Izzy. It would blast my career to the front pages. *New York Times, Wall Street Journal,* on and on. But I promised the man in the cave I wouldn't tell where this place was located."

"You what? Didn't he end up letting you take the pictures? You don't take pictures to keep them secret. He's got to know that."

"I forced him, Izzy. After I heard him mooing and moaning

with his busted hand, I took the opportunity to snap as many photos as I could. I kind of stole those pictures. And doesn't he have the right to hold the place as a private place of worship or something? I mean, I did have this strong feeling, a kind of feeling of embarrassment. You know, you just don't walk into somebody's living room and start clicking pictures while the owner tries to shove you out. I wouldn't do that in New York City to anybody, but there I was taking shots of this guy's place and him yelling at me to stop. And then he started making the case for the cave being a holy place, and I had no idea what that even meant."

"And what is a holy place?" she says. "What is an icon? A picture of a nonexistent god."

"Not to him."

"So he's wrong. Facts are facts, Philly." She leans into him and squeezes his thigh. "Show me more of the shots, crazy Philip."

He clicks through thirty or forty images. She is rapt. She moans at some of the photos, points out details, admires the lighting, the angles, the coloration. He can see she's getting more excited. "Philip, this is, like, perfection, babe. They'll love this!"

"But Izzy. It's more than what you're saying: 'Angles, cobalt blues, sparkling whites, glitterey golds.' Come on, doesn't that face kind of strike you funny?"

"Funny?"

"Strange. I mean maybe the way the face looks out of that cave wall, coming right out of the rock. It hit me in the gut, Izzy. Spoke to me. Still does. That solemn, serious face looking right back at me. Black eyes. It took my breath away, Izzy. Stopped my heart. I think it had the same effect on the Lebanese guy, because it seemed to stall him out. He just stood in the shadows rooted to the floor—even though he must have seen that same sight a thousand times. And that face, Izzy. It wasn't staring at me like I was staring at it. It looked at me. At me, Philip. Not surprised at all to see me, like he was expecting me these thousand years and more."

"Philip. It's a mosaic, pieces of rock stuck on a cave wall."

"I know, I know. Come on! Whap! Nose to the wire. I'm just trying to give you that first impression, for God's sake. That first shock. It kind of mystified me, and I had to get a picture, had to get my head around this thing, so I grabbed for my camera and snapped a pic, then another. I just kept snapping pics like the photo addict I am."

"Of course you did. It's beautiful. Intricate. Look at the way the little stones fit together, almost like an impressionist painting or something. Philip, you could do a whole gallery exposition just on this one image! So many shots. Such a strong figure and face. Do you know what the letters on the book stand for?"

"They're Greek for 'Who was. Who is. Who is to come.'"

"Okay."

"It's a quote from the biblical book of Revelation."

She looks up at him.

"It means that he is God."

"Interesting."

"It is." He slides back in the seat and drops his head on the backrest and stares at the ceiling. "I felt weird about it all. Have felt weird about taking those pics, Izzy. Like I said, it was like walking unannounced into somebody's home and flashing fifty pics and having every intention of publishing the whole damn thing. That can't be right."

"So? We have a right to publish great art, Philly." She starts absently brushing her hair, looking out the window. "For the education of the world. For, like, filling in the history of that part of the world. For the gorgeous art. I can think of a dozen reasons you should show these to your editors. Let them make the decision." She looks back at him and smiles. "We've got to start thinking about our family, Philip. Think what this could mean."

He catches her eyes, sits up and turns his eyes to the seat in front of them.

"You could barely afford these train tickets, Philip. You're young, and photographers are, like, a dime a dozen. You need this, babe. My teaching sixth graders makes no money. *We* need this. If we have any kids, they'll need the income. What happens when I take time off teaching to have a baby?"

"So how would you like it if some Lebanese guy walked into your parents' apartment and started snapping pictures?"

"They have no art in their apartment."

"Thanks a lot. They've got some of my photos."

"This is different, Philip. You know that. This is history we're talking about."

"So we have the right to steal history."

"You're not stealing anything! You're taking pictures!"

Over the next hour, the argument burns and flares, smokes and sputters.

"For three months, I've been researching this, Izzy. Thinking about this, grinding it around in my skull like stones in a canister. Over and over again, around and around, day after day, night after goddamned night."

"The crickets."

"God almighty, yes! The damned, stomping cricket!"

"Crickets don't stomp." She sighs and looks out the window.

"Izzy, I want to stomp it, squash it. Stomp the little bastard! Get this over with!"

After the train leaves Philadelphia, they get up and walk the aisle to the dining car and eat their dinners in silence. He can see that the stones are grinding in her head too.

"And why," she says, looking up from her coffee, "should you, like, sacrifice our future to your jumpy conscience, to a twingey feeling?" Her dark eyes are intense.

"And what is a conscience?" he asks looking down into his cup of black coffee.

"It's a personal feeling," she says. "And why would you sacrifice our success to a little personal feeling? My mom and dad are, like, dead set against me sleeping with you, good little Catholics that they are, but that hasn't stopped us, has it?"

"This is more than that. That guy's life is in this. And look, morals have got to be more than my attitude or your attitude or an emotional reaction, a twinge."

"Well, what are they?"

"A principle is more than a feeling. There is such a thing as right and wrong, or you wouldn't try to justify your position with reasons about the rights of the world to see the icon, about our right to publish the photographs."

"Okay. I'll buy that. There might be principles, but people tend to make them up as they go along, don't you think?"

"Some do."

"Philip, this is not just about me and you. If you became a well-known photographer, think what it would do for our families. Maybe my mom could stop cleaning houses, for Christ's sake. I hate that my mama has to do that. My papa is almost 62. Maybe he could even retire."

"I know, I know, Izzy. I want to. You know I do. But that cave in Lebanon shook me. I sometimes had the same feeling in those little French chapels: the stark crucifixes and stone saints, the candles burning."

"So it's the lighting that got to you. You're a photographer; you care about lighting."

"I told the guy the icon looked better in lamplight. He then got up and lit a half dozen oil lamps that were on little stone ledges or shelves cut into the cave walls. I think his hand *was* broken. It took him a while to strike the matches with his left hand. So meanwhile, I was setting up my tripod, and I was thinking about this guy's dirt-poor life in Detroit running car washes. Can you imagine? With all this gold in the cave, an absolute fortune in gold, he was working for some guy running car washes! Meanwhile, he was lighting the candles, and I was setting the aperture on old Betsy, and this beautiful smell was in the cave. Must have been something in the lamps. I got those last thirty shots without using the flash. The first one I showed you was without the flash."

"That guy lit the lamps for you? He wanted you to see it in that light, take those pictures? So you had some kind of mystical reaction. That's natural enough: pretty lamp light, a dark place, strange scents. All this after the shock of the storm and a near-death experience. You shouldn't be surprised by an emotional reaction. And look, you're not stealing the gold from anyone! You're, like, giving it back to the world by way of photographs."

"I told him that very thing, but I'm not sure my selfishness should trump his selfishness."

"You're giving it to the world, Philip! A great discovery. A revelation. Like finding the Dead Sea Scrolls!"

"Strange, but it feels to me like I stumbled into a different reality, a new world."

She arches her eyebrows. "A new world? You're not Columbus."

"Columbus's expedition turned out well for the natives, didn't it?"

"Come on, Philip! So you think Columbus should have turned around and sailed back to Spain and sworn his sailors to secrecy to protect the natives?"

"Your dad and mom are descendants of those natives, Izzy. And I don't have to swear a crew to secrecy. Only you."

"Philip. I want this for you. You love photography. Maybe us natives can actually benefit for a change. That icon had to be made for a reason, not to be hidden away forever."

He looks down into his cup of cold coffee. Picks it up and drains the last of it.

They get up and return to their seats in the passenger car.

She stares out the window. After a minute, she says, "You won't take my advice."

"This is beyond you and me."

"You and me aren't beyond this."

"I love you, Izzy. You're the best thing that's ever happened to me. But I can't be shoved on this one."

"But you don't know what's right; otherwise you wouldn't have asked for my advice."

"Good point."

The sun sets, and the train rumbles on, stopping at stations, people getting off and others finding seats. The train is rolling into Ohio. He keeps looking across the aisle and out the far window at the passing groves of darkening trees, the occasional town and water tower, listening to the triple call of the train engine as it approaches the many, many crossroads, the stones grinding now in his stomach.

"After all the photos, I packed up and hightailed it out of that cave. I was afraid that guy might have a change of heart and grab old Betsy, or maybe me and Betsy both, and heave us over that cliff."

"Of course. I'm so glad you got out."

"It was still cloudy when I got out of the cave, but the storm had passed. Just a light rain. My mind, my whole body was full of my success, Izzy. Of finding and photographing a sure-fire success. I edged along that ledge and scrambled up the washout and took off running, slipping and sliding, then running down the trail. I was shouting to the clouds. I was leaping. I knew this would be a tremendous hit."

"Absolutely. You were right."

"But on the plane flight over the Atlantic, I had second thoughts. Started thinking again of that Lebanese guy's concerns. Started wondering if I'd misplayed this. I started thinking I should have stayed. Opened my ears for a change. But I kept on babbling to that guy. Arguing, bringing up this, bringing up that. Never shut my mouth but for the minutes I was setting up Betsy. I don't even know his name. . . . I don't even know the man's name."

"He wanted you out."

"I should have waited. Shut my mouth. He had a perspective on this I wasn't getting."

She glances at him and returns her eyes to the window and the passing shadows.

"I just don't know," he says. "I feel like I'm about to betray this guy and his sacred place. It's serious, even if you don't see it that way."

"But you don't believe that shit, Philip. Why should we take it so seriously?"

"It bothers me. I'm in over my head."

"So let your editors make the decision."

"No. It's my call. I'm responsible."

"Are you actually afraid? You think God who missed you with the lightning bolts will zap little Philip for being a bad boy in the cave?"

"Maybe I *should* be afraid . . . maybe I should be."

"Damn you, Philip!" She turns to look out the window.

The light outside is gone. Occasionally there are passing pin pricks of light from a farm house or a scattered cluster of lights from a passing town; sometimes she can hear the triple call of the train engine in the night, and she listens to the rushing rumble of the iron wheels and feels it in her body, but all she can really see in the window are their two reflections: a troubled anger written across her own forehead and face and, when she leans back, his hard head leaning toward his laptop, his finger tapping through the images, the colored lights on his face, the wonder in his eyes as if he is reading and rereading and reading again some new verse of an ancient and powerful rhyme.